KILLIAN

The Mavericks, Book 15

Dale Mayer

KILLIAN: THE MAVERICKS, BOOK 15
Dale Mayer
Valley Publishing Ltd.

Copyright © 2021

All rights reserved. Except for use in any review, the reproduction or utilization of this work in whole or in part by any electronic, mechanical or other means, now known or hereafter invented, including xerography, photocopying and recording, or in any information storage or retrieval system, is forbidden without the written permission of the publisher.

This is a work of fiction. Names, characters, places, brands, media, and incidents are either the product of the author's imagination or are used fictitiously. Any resemblance to actual events, locales, or persons, living or dead, is entirely coincidental.

ISBN-13: 978-1-773363-74-5
Print Edition

Books in This Series:

Kerrick, Book 1
Griffin, Book 2
Jax, Book 3
Beau, Book 4
Asher, Book 5
Ryker, Book 6
Miles, Book 7
Nico, Book 8
Keane, Book 9
Lennox, Book 10
Gavin, Book 11
Shane, Book 12
Diesel, Book 13
Jerricho, Book 14
Killian, Book 15
Hatch, Book 16
The Mavericks, Books 1–2
The Mavericks, Books 3–4
The Mavericks, Books 5–6
The Mavericks, Books 7–8
The Mavericks, Books 9–10
The Mavericks, Books 11–12

About This Book

What happens when the very men—trained to make the hard decisions—come up against the rules and regulations that hold them back from doing what needs to be done? They either stay and work within the constraints given to them or they walk away. Only now, for a select few, they have another option:

The Mavericks. A covert black ops team that steps up and break all the rules … but gets the job done.

Welcome to a new military romance series by *USA Today* best-selling author Dale Mayer. A series where you meet new friends and just might get to meet old ones too in this raw and compelling look at the men who keep us safe every day from the darkness where they operate—and live—in the shadows … until someone special helps them step into the light.

Killian is called up to retrieve a woman who's been kidnapped, then escaped, only to be captured again. With a sketchy SOS coming in, Killian's tracking her from Vancouver to the far reaches of the Yukon Territory in Canada, right next door to Alaska, where the intel finally stops.

The apple of her father's eye, Stacey was a late gift in his life. But, when it counted, he wasn't there for her, leaving her alone and unprotected. On the run from her abusive husband, she's kidnapped a second time by a seasoned negotiator, who can see she's in trouble. Only he plans to auction her off to the highest bidder.

With several threads running together on this mission, Killian must find the predator in the middle and take him out, or Stacey will never be safe again.

Sign up to be notified of all Dale's releases here!

https://smarturl.it/DaleNews

PROLOGUE

KILLIAN NORDSTROM WALKED along the beach, picked up a piece of driftwood, and threw it out into the ocean. He had come for a run, and now he was staying because, well, it was just so damn beautiful. He stood for a long moment, smiling at the world around him. When he turned to head back, he stopped because a figure on the cliff watched him. He walked up to see his sister. "Hey, sis. How's life?"

"It would be better," she said, "if it weren't for these phone calls." She held out her own phone. He looked at it and asked, "Who is it?" But she didn't answer, just thrust her phone at him. He grabbed her phone, frowning, putting it to his ear.

"It's me, Jerricho," he said. "You didn't answer your phone."

"I left it in my room," he said. "It's just been so beautiful here on the beach."

"I'm enjoying a different beach," Jerricho said.

"You're not that far away," he said.

"Nope, but you will be soon."

At that, Killian stilled. "Where am I going?"

"How do you feel about Vancouver Island?"

He frowned. "Canada?"

"Yeah, Canada. And a woman who's got an issue."

"Yeah, but that's not exactly pirate country."

"Nope, it isn't, but a woman was kidnapped from a transport ship, and, when they got to the Vancouver docks, she escaped somehow. Even though the longshoremen were more stunned, I think, than anything, she sent out an SOS for help on Vancouver Island."

"How the hell did she go from Vancouver to Vancouver Island?"

"I don't know," he said. "And her story is a little bit farfetched. However, we have to consider it legit because of who she is."

"And who is she?"

"She's the daughter of the New York governor, who just retired."

"Daughter?"

"Yes, she was one of those late-in-life children. He was fifty-five when she was born."

"Wow, that has to be tough."

"The apple of his eye. She has been traveling the world. She's a chef and was picked up and tossed onto an overseas carrier, where she somehow ended up in Vancouver. Now she's lost on Vancouver Island."

"But Vancouver Island's tiny," he said. "That's a hard place to get lost in. Besides, Canadians? … How hard can it be?"

"One SOS came from Vancouver Island. But the one after that came from farther up the coast."

"Alaska?"

"It didn't come from that far north, but we're afraid that's the direction she's going or traveling, so it could very well be where she ends up."

"Did she ask for help? Did she ask for a pickup? What

the hell's going on?"

"She sent out the SOS, but the last one came in as a kidnapper's note for ransom."

"Shit. So did they find her again? Is that the deal?"

"Or somebody else found her and decided to take advantage of her circumstances."

"I hate people sometimes," he said.

"In this case, the governor doesn't have much influence, outside of the fact that he's still connected. I'm not sure what could be the issue here, but he did say that her ex-husband is a possible suspect."

"Why?"

"Apparently he was involved in a few things that weren't quite kosher, and she left him. As part of her leverage to make sure that he didn't take her to the cleaners and that he left her alive, she apparently took some material with her."

"Uh-oh," Killian said, "that's never smart."

"No, never smart. In this case, it may have backfired, but apparently he's quite an asshole, and she needed something in order to feel like she could get out of the situation safely."

"The governor couldn't do it?"

"Father and husband were really close. Until she went to her father with all the evidence on her hubby, so now her father believes her."

"Well, that's something. Isn't it a little bit too late?"

"Which is why he's pulled in all the chips to see if he can get her back. He feels responsible for not having given her his trust and security back then."

"How long has she been missing?"

"The ransom note came in an hour ago."

"Shit." He looked one last time at the beauty surrounding him and said, "I'm packed."

3

"Good," he said, "because, if you walk up that cliff, you'll find yourself at the road, where a car's waiting for you."

"And my bag?"

"It's already in the trunk," he said. "Have a nice trip." And, with that, Jerricho hung up.

His sister looked at him and said, "I gather you're leaving?"

"Sorry, sis. I figured I was only here for a couple days."

She shrugged. "Honestly I'm just glad to have seen you that long," she murmured. "Go off and save the world. It's what you're good at."

He smiled and said, "How did you know?"

"I heard part of that conversation," she said. "And, if she needs a place to relax afterward, she's always welcome here."

"That's just because you think I'll come home with her."

"Hearing the little bit you've told me about the company you work for," she said, "I wouldn't be at all surprised."

"What do you mean?"

"Haven't they all come back with partners?" she said. "I'll hardly be upset if this is your next mission, and you come back with one too."

He looked at her askance. "What? And lose my freedom?"

She snorted. "Pretty sure that freedom doesn't matter one damn bit to you," she said.

He grinned as they walked up, and he pointed to the vehicle and said, "There's my ride."

She nodded, gave him a big kiss on the cheek, and said, "Go save the world."

"Maybe not the world," he said, "just one woman."

"Make sure it's the right one," she said, with a big grin.

And he hopped into the vehicle and took off.

CHAPTER 1

KILLIAN NORDSTROM EXITED his vehicle, parked in the hotel's outdoor parking space, and stretched. Seemed like he'd been traveling for hours, and, of course, he had. But now he was here. He yawned, reached behind him into the car, and grabbed his bag, shutting the door this time. He headed to the entrance, then sauntered to the front desk, where he quickly checked in. Nothing fancy about this hotel. But, as the intel had been flowing fast since his departure from California, this trip to Whitehorse in Canada's Yukon Territory had been nothing short of a series of fast military hops, with multiple connections, finally hooking him up with a rented vehicle.

All he cared about now was that he had made it to his destination. In his room he quickly dropped his bag, walked to the window, and checked out the view, noting how close the trails and parks and the wilds of Mother Nature were to this town. He was in need of a good solid meal, preferably something with a lot of red meat. As he walked back into the reception area, he asked for the closest restaurant where he could get a steak. Apparently just down the block and around the corner. With that, he tossed back a smile of thanks and headed out, donning a hat and sunglasses.

In the dead heat of summer, he knew, once he hit the bush, that black flies were everywhere. They were almost as big as the bloody grizzlies, he was sure. But he would take animal predators over people any day. The animals were predictable, their motivations simple. But when it came to people? Well, things were never quite so simple. He knew that he looked a bit scruffy, but he didn't want to look too good. He didn't want to draw any attention to himself; so looking like he was just passing through was fine with him.

As he walked to the restaurant, he studied his surroundings, getting a feel for the atmosphere. A few people milled about—nobody suspicious or too interested in him—and a little bit of traffic, but not like in the big cities he was used to. The air here was fresh, had a cleanliness to it that he hadn't really been expecting. Also a mugginess that was hard to ignore, no matter where you were in the world. When that heat hit the muggy air, it was forced down onto the town and ended up as this stickiness that soaked through your clothing with every step you took.

As soon as he walked inside the restaurant, the blast of cold air-conditioning hit him, and he froze in the spot for a long moment, just enjoying it.

The hostess walked over and smiled. "AC is one of the best inventions in the world."

He nodded with a smile. "As is heat."

She laughed out loud at that. "It all depends on which day and the time of the year," she said, "and I'd change my comment to match."

He nodded. "Table for one," he said. "I need a big steak tonight."

"I think we can do that," she said, as he followed her to the back of the room.

She gave him a small table for two and asked, "Is this okay?"

"It's perfect," he said. "I don't really want anybody to join me because I'm not feeling terribly social."

"Not a problem," she said. "I'll bring you some coffee. Or do you want something stronger?"

"A beer sounds great," he said instantly. "Also do you have any bread? French, sourdough, something along that line?"

"Sure," she said, as she quickly disappeared, leaving him to settle into place.

His phone buzzed. He pulled it out, took a look, and noted that lovely empty black text box. He never really quite knew who was on the other end. When he didn't check in on his designated arrival time, he was prompted to do so.

He typed one word. **Arrived.** Then he put his phone off to the side, as the waitress returned with a glass of cold beer topped by a beautiful foam. He picked it up and took a good slug. "Thank you," he said in appreciation. "In this heat there's nothing like it."

She nodded as she also put down a wooden board, with a small loaf of bread on it and a tub of butter. "Now," she said, "here's your menu."

He waved away the menu. "I want a medium-rare steak, a baked potato, and something green on the side—either a salad or some steamed vegetables."

"Got you covered," she said, and she turned and walked away quickly.

He dug into the bread and had half of it gone before she returned with a large platter.

He whistled appreciatively. "Now this is what I'm talking about." In front of him was a huge steak, an equally large baked potato, and just a little bit of green beans. Normally he liked his greens just fine, but, right now, he was all about red meat. He cut into it with a smile because not only was it a good portion but it was cooked just the way he liked it.

In other words, this would be a hell of a meal. He dug in, and the only thing that interrupted him was ordering a second beer halfway through. By the time he was done with his meal, he pushed back his empty plate with a happy sigh.

The waitress returned to clear his table.

He smiled and murmured, "Thanks. That was a great meal."

"I'm glad you liked it," she said, with a bright smile, as she quickly collected the remaining dishes.

He got up and walked to the front.

She met him there and quickly gave him the bill. After settling up, including a sizable tip, he headed out. By now it was a little bit cooler but not a whole lot. He checked his surroundings. *Empty.* He pulled out his phone, still nothing from anybody, which suited him fine. He had a delivery coming to the hotel, another reason he needed to get going. Hopefully it was already there. He didn't want even the courier to see him. The less people who did made his job easier. But in this small town? Killian feared the waitress and the hotel clerk were two people too many.

He strolled along the street, carefully checking if anybody was out, if anybody was paying any attention, but the place was dead. Like dead-dead. As in, nobody around—nobody. It was past normal work hours, and they'd all gone home, somewhere. Wherever that was, Killian didn't know. The place was seriously quiet. And that worked for him. It was much easier to take care of business when he didn't have a constant audience. He passed the reception desk and headed upstairs to his room. He entered it quietly, and, as expected, the parcel had arrived.

He smiled. He did like doing business, where you put in a request and had it delivered as soon as possible, without arguments or even conversation. Somehow the Mavericks always managed to get what he needed. It was a good system, even if it left things a little on the creepy side—especially if you were a team person, always looking for the other half of your team. Killian hadn't expected to be alone on this op, but, even as he turned to open the bag, he heard a noise, and he froze, his hand going to his shoulder holster.

A man stepped out of the bathroom, grinning in an almost friendly way.

Killian stared at him and murmured, "I almost shot you. Who are you, and why are you here?"

"*Nah*, I knew you wouldn't shoot without asking questions," said the relaxed man in front of him.

Killian studied the stranger's face. Tall and swarthy with dark hair, yet somehow vaguely familiar. "I know you, but I don't know you."

"Surgery," he said. "A hell of a lot of it."

"Hatch?" Killian asked in shock, his gun hand dropping by his side as recognition slammed into him.

A real smile crept out. He nodded. "Hatch Collar, in the flesh. Your sight is still pretty decent, considering you recognized me through the damage."

"Jesus," he said. "I didn't even know you were back to work."

"I'm not really," Hatch said. "At least not the normal route. The Mavericks suit me better."

"Last I heard, you were severely injured," Killian said cautiously. "As in, never to return to active duty."

"I was, but now I'm fully recovered and back in fighting form." His voice held a slight edge, as if daring anyone to argue the point.

"And you're working for the Mavericks?" He was stilled stunned at his old friend's appearance.

"Yes," he said. "Unless you veto my participation."

Immediately Killian shook his head. "Oh, hell no. You made it this far, so you go all the way. You deserve it."

"I don't deserve or need another chance," he said tersely. "I'm just fine as I am. I just thought maybe I could do more to help the messed-up world out there."

"It's even worse now," Killian said. He studied Hatch's face, the scars visible, even though everything possible had been done to minimize them. "What happened to you? I heard stories but—"

"I entered a house as it was bombed. The ceiling came down on top of me, while I was trying to get the rest of the team out."

"And you got them out, as I recall."

"I did, but, of course, you're not the same afterward. The military didn't want to keep me in the same line of work, especially after I'd been through something like that. They offered me retirement or a desk job."

"Not our style," Killian replied, as he studied the man he used to know, and yet he looked so very different. "It's a bit of a shock to see you."

"I'm half waiting for you to call it in," he said, with a careless shrug.

"Oh, God, I know what happened was terrible, but, hey, I also know you saved your team," he said. "Nobody else could have done what you did. I'll be happy to have you watch my back any day."

And, with that, a little bit more of the tension held in Hatch's shoulders sagged, and he began to relax. "Oh, well, I don't know what to—thanks for that," he said, blowing out a big exhale. "I ended up with a chip on my shoulder, even though I thought I had already dealt with all this shit."

"A word to the wise," Killian said. "We never get all this shit dealt with."

At that, Hatch burst out laughing. "Isn't that the truth," he said. "So what are we doing here? Where are we at?"

"Supposed to pick up a woman who was kidnapped, escaped, and then was kidnapped again. We don't know if it's the same kidnapper or if it's a completely different issue."

"Surely a woman can't have such bad luck that she would end up with two different kidnapping issues," Hatch said.

"You wouldn't think so, wouldn't you?" he said. "But, on the other hand, this gal apparently has bad luck, all the way around."

"Interesting. And you've just come back from dinner, and I've already eaten." He sat down in a chair and said, "What kind of details do we have?"

Killian quickly shared what little he had.

"And a second ransom note?"

"No, not yet," he said. "But he demanded a drop in the Yukon. Which is why we're here now."

"That makes no sense," Hatch said.

"I know," Killian replied. "I told Jerricho it sounded like a setup."

"It does, indeed," Hatch said, with a frown. "So … we're just waiting for him to make contact then?"

"Yes."

"And do we know for sure that he has the woman?"

"I'll be asking him for proof, if he calls."

"Great, so we really don't know a whole lot."

"We really don't."

"A trip for nothing, maybe, huh?"

"God no, if there's even a chance to save the woman's life, it's worth the trip, but, at the same time, we just don't know if we really have a case here."

"That would be great, since it would mean that maybe she wasn't in trouble," Hatch said. "So the first kidnapping was the husband?"

"I can't say that for certain," Killian cautioned. "I can say that he is looking like a good suspect."

"Asshole," he said. "Why can't people just get divorced?"

"That would make the world a whole lot easier," he murmured, "but it doesn't seem to be that way, does it?"

"Nope, so I guess we'll just sit here, waiting, huh?"

Killian pointed at the bag. "Did you bring this?"

"Yep. As per your instructions."

"Let's stash this, connect with the bosses, and see who all knows something." Killian took off a grate in the wall behind an oversize chair, settling the bag inside, then replaced the grate.

"I don't quite understand how it is that we have bosses," Hatch said, "but we don't really have bosses."

"Basically the last guy you looked after becomes your handler. So the next mission would be yours, and I'd be your handler."

"So my boss?"

"No, the decisions would be yours. This time we'll make them together, you and me in this instance," he said. "It's very much a two-man operation."

"Did your last job go okay?" Hatch asked Killian.

"Can't say it was wonderful, but it turned out fine."

"Good," Hatch said. "So let's hope this one does too."

Killian sat down with a laptop and quickly opened it up, logged in on a secure video connection to check on any updates.

Jerricho appeared onscreen and responded, "No update. The father is worried and pressing for action."

"What did you tell him?"

"Told him that you two were involved and had boots on the ground."

"Probably not enough information for him to feel comfortable."

"Well, if it was your daughter, would you?"

"Uh, nope. I need more information on the drop."

"Did they give you the address earlier?"

"Yep, and I took a hotel only a few blocks away from it. Man, this place is dead," Killian said. "I don't see any street cameras, none at all."

"Check the hotel and see if any outdoor cameras are there," Jerricho said.

"I'll take a walk down the street in a little bit and see if there's any sign of her."

"Probably won't be," Jerricho said.

"I still don't like anything about this," Killian replied.

"Neither do I," Jerricho said, "but we're out of options. This is the hand we're dealt, and this is the hand we'll have to play."

"Still doesn't mean I have to like it," he said.

"How's your partner?"

"He's perfect," Killian said readily. "I've known Hatch since, well, since a long time ago. I just didn't realize he was back in the game."

"He asked to come back in. He was referred to the Mavericks."

"Good choice," he said. "I'm always happy to have him on my team."

"Right, he's got that innate sense of honor, which is just not there in so many guys. Let me know what you find when you take your walk. Find every camera on this block, on every block for a one-mile radius around there because, if something goes wrong, we'll need to track those assholes."

"Right." As he went to log off, Killian quickly added, "Hey, let me know where the sewers and any underground tunnels are in this ungodly and beautiful place," Killian requested.

Jerricho laughed.

"It's a nice small town, and, so far, I have absolutely nothing against it," Killian said. "Also lots of fresh air, so that's a big plus. But, if anything is underground, with any potential hidden exits, I need to know."

"Okay, I'll check that for you. Go, take your walk outside, and make sure you're not seen."

He logged off and looked over at Hatch. "Want to go for a walk?"

Hatch nodded. "I so do."

"Good, except you should look a little bit more homeless or unseen."

"Yes, I agree. I did see a couple street people when wandering through town earlier," Hatch said. "But not very many."

"And that's a huge plus for this place. They take care of their own."

"Yeah, either they haven't made it up here, there aren't that many per capita, or they're holed up in some other area."

"Yes, you'd think by one of the waterways would be a

likely spot for them to congregate," he said.

"You'd think so. For me, I'll stay in the shadows."

Hatch left first, and Killian followed, locking up behind them, each going in a different direction. They would take completely different routes, checking out the neighborhood. Then they would reconvene and share notes.

As Killian wandered about town, he sent a message to Jerricho. **We have ventured out, and the place is completely empty. Nobody on the streets at all.**

Anybody watching you, like in the windows or the doorsteps? By the way, no underground tunnels.

Good. One thing to ignore. Nobody at all. Not even a parked car. He sent the messages as he walked. **I mean, I've been in a lot of small towns, but a weird atmosphere hangs around this one. I can't explain it.**

And that's probably you, he messaged back.

Maybe, and maybe it's not. He walked on but still found no vehicles parked on the side streets or the main drag.

He knew it was a Monday and was well past dinnertime, but he hadn't expected this level of deadness as he walked toward the rendezvous spot, which was a wooded area just off the town itself.

He checked his watch for the time frame to hook up with Hatch. He thought he caught sight of Hatch as he crossed a block and headed around the corner. But, as Killian kept looking, he found no sign of him again. Either Hatch was as good as he had always been or somebody else was out here, playing games. Considering the drop-off point was nearby, exchanging the woman for the money that had been delivered to his room, somebody working with the kidnapper must be out here, scouting the area at least.

Before coming here, Killian had dyed his hair, had shaved off his beard, wore colored contacts, and carried a hat to avoid street cams, so he didn't look like his normal self anymore. Hatch was already in a disguise. It just blew Killian away how different the man looked. But then again, burns like that and skin grafts, they weren't kind. Hatch still looked good, but, no doubt about it, he didn't look the same. So trying to ID Killian or Hatch out here using facial recognition wouldn't work. That was a huge bonus right now. Killian made a single pass again and headed back toward the hotel.

On his second pass, he felt that creepy sensation of being followed. He was still too early for their rendezvous, and he casually walked past the hotel. Then, as soon as he felt he was clear, he swept around the alleyway and came up on the other block and did a quick dash through until he came up on the other side of the hotel, where he raced up the front steps and then walked sedately through the entrance.

That was the problem with this hotel; it had one main exit. The back one was apparently closed off, and that had made him very suspicious when he had first arrived. But the hotel manager had said they were just doing some work on the locks. And, of course, that was always questionable.

When he got back to the room, he found Hatch already there. "See anything?" he asked Hatch.

"I wanted to, yet, no," he said. "But I sure felt it."

"Yeah, I did too. I couldn't make out anyone, but they're around." Killian quickly opened his laptop and brought up the secure message screen in the Mavericks' chat box. **Did you confirm regarding the locks in the hotel?**

Yes, they were damaged, early this morning. New locks installed.

Did you check out the lock installer?
Yes, he's clean.
Still, it sounds suspicious.
I know. I don't like anything about this.

Killian looked up and quickly explained the lock issue to Hatch.

Hatch said, "I don't like anything about that."

"I know, and it's the back exit too. I'm thinking we should disable the lock."

"Otherwise it'll be locked to stop us from getting out," Hatch said, nodding.

"That would be my take on it."

With that, Hatch got up and quickly slipped out of the room.

Killian sent a message back to Jerricho. **Hatch's gone to take a look at the lock.**

Good, he replied. **Ready for the drop?**

Yes. Killian retrieved the bag and picked up the small backpack with the $50,000 inside, then messaged Jerricho. **Not a whole lot of money for a woman's life.**

And I'm not sure she'll even be there. That's the next problem.

Oh, she'll likely be there, but they probably won't give her to us. They could keep doing this. What's to stop them?

You. And, with that, Jerricho logged off.

STACEY EDGEWATER GROANED behind the blindfold and the mouth gag. Her hands were tied at her back, and her feet were scrunched up, also tied together. She was in the trunk of a car. At least, that was her best guess. When the lid opened, and she was roughly pulled into a sitting position, the gag was yanked off her mouth, and a bottle was held up to her lips. She drank thirstily, spilling half of it down her front. She didn't care; it was water, and she was parched.

All too soon the bottle was pulled away. She said, "Bastard."

A chuckle erupted.

"Is Max paying you? Or is that you, Max?" she asked in a hard tone. "Either way, this is a bit much, even for you."

Another chuckle came, and that was it; the gag was secured over her mouth. She was shoved back down, but the trunk lid wasn't closed. She tried to relax, trying to get the fresh air that she needed to calm down. Being in a trunk was just painful. And terrifying.

As she lay here, she listened for other sounds but heard nothing. She couldn't ask questions; she couldn't see anything. She'd been in a nightmare scenario for days—several nightmare scenarios. Not only had she been kidnapped and escaped but then had been attacked and kidnapped a second time—and she didn't know if the two events were connected. Of the two, this second kidnapper terrified her more than anything she'd been through yet.

He'd sliced her leg badly almost immediately, telling her how she may have escaped her first kidnapper, but she wouldn't get away from him. Otherwise he didn't talk to her. He'd let her out to go to the bathroom—always somewhere deserted, where no one would ask questions. For the few times he'd given her water and a sandwich, she'd relished the food and water but had also appreciated when the gag came off. The blindfold ... had yet to be removed. She had no idea who this man was. She didn't recognize his voice or his smell, but that meant little after days of captivity.

Apparently they'd completed the ferry journey to Victoria, BC, as she overheard what was probably a ferry announcement, but he'd driven to another terminal and had caught a much smaller ferry crossing—fewer vehicle noises, in her perception—back to the mainland maybe but kept driving, farther up the coast, she imagined, as it felt colder to her. They were in Whitehorse now, which she only knew from overhearing a phone call her kidnapper had. *Whitehorse.* A place she'd never been, had never imagined going to, and had never contemplated under these circumstances.

She hadn't been given a chance to ask why or who, nothing. All she could think about was that this was all happening because she had left her husband. Her second kidnapper had confirmed that Max had been responsible for the first kidnapping. It was too much to assume that two people hated her as much as Max. She groaned, as she shifted again.

"Shut up," her kidnapper said.

She sighed and tried to mumble around the gag in her mouth.

A hard clip to the side of her head sent stars spinning through her gaze and tears to her eyes. She choked back sobs.

"It'll all be over in a few minutes," he said.

She wondered *what* would be over. She hadn't been asked for anything, so obviously none of the kidnappers knew she had taken something from her husband. So was her husband even involved? And why? Her mind reeled with questions. She was a marketer, not some business analyst, so, when it came to analyzing this mess, she couldn't make two and two come together. None of these kidnappings made any sense.

If her husband wanted to get rid of her, why not simply

sign the divorce papers? Or, even if he meant to kill her, why didn't he toss her into a cargo ship, to be thrown overboard in the middle of some ocean? That would have been a much surer death—or disappearance—than this nightmare was turning out to be.

Her head was smacked again, only this time, a little bit lighter. She rolled over, trying to take deep breaths, but it was hard with the gag in her mouth. She heard an odd exclamation, and then the gag was pulled off.

"Calm down," the man snapped. "It'll be over soon. I told you that."

"*What* will be over soon?" she asked.

"The sale," he replied. "I'm selling you." At that, she froze, and he burst into raucous laughter. "Not like that! Jesus," he said. "I'm ransoming you, let's put it that way."

"Why?" she whispered in horror.

"Because somebody wants you, and I figured that, if one person wants you, somebody else would probably want you more."

"So I'll go to the highest bidder?"

"Yep," he said. "Makes sense to me."

"*Great*," she said. "Do I get to know which side is buying me?"

"Well, both of them offered," he said. "I'm seeing how I can make that work to my advantage."

"Oh, shit," she said. "You're selling me to both? You're hoping that they either kill each other off or that you'll take one out or that you'll just get the money from both and run."

"Yep," he said smugly. "It's worked a couple times, so no reason it won't work this time."

She sank back into the trunk and groaned again.

"Why are you groaning all the time?"

"Because you're a fool," she said bluntly, and she immediately got smacked across the side of the head again, enduring more pain.

"Don't call me that," he said in a tight voice.

"One of these days," she murmured, her eyes closed against the agony as she struggled to get the words out, "somebody will get you at your game."

"But not today," he snapped. "I've already got payment from one, and I'm picking up payment on the other."

"Shit," she said. "So how do you decide who I go to?"

"I don't really care," he said, "but the ones today want proof of life."

"I see. And the other one didn't?"

"Let's just say that the other one preferred you didn't come out of this alive."

"That would be my husband."

He burst out laughing. "You should figure out how to be a better wife, or this is how you end up," he said. "Do you know how many husbands try to get rid of their wives?"

"I wouldn't be at all surprised," she said. "It's a sad world out there."

"It is, if you're on the bottom of the mess," he said. "Otherwise, it's a pretty nice world out there for those of us at the top."

"Yeah," she said, "and it sucks when guys like you do bullshit like this, for piece-of-shit husbands who don't want to just get a divorce like everybody else."

"Well, you got out of whatever trouble you were in and tried for freedom," he said. "Fortunately I found you, and now he's paying me good money to make sure you don't survive."

"And you'll follow through on that?" she asked in a hoarse whisper.

"Well, I mean, I've already taken his money for the job."

"And the other one who's paying?"

"Well, I'm ransoming you back to your dad," he said.

Her heart sank because, of course, her dad would do this, putting him in danger as well. "So you'll take his money but not give him his daughter back," she said bitterly.

"Well, there can only be one winner," he murmured.

"That's not true," she said. "You could just take the money and run and leave me alive."

"And piss off your husband? If he was willing to pay to have you killed, what do you think he'd plan for me?"

"I'd be up for that outcome," she said, with a snort.

"I'm sure you would," he said, "but I don't really want anybody like him coming after me."

"No, of course not," she said. "You're obviously weak because he only comes after people weaker than him." She grimaced, waiting for another blow to the head.

Instead the man was silent for a long moment, and then he chuckled. "So you do understand him. It might be fun to con him too."

"It probably would be," she said, "but I don't have any money to buy my way out of this, and that's the only language you seem to understand."

"Not true," he said. "I understand all kinds of languages, but I don't have time for that now. I have to give proof of life to somebody before I get paid."

"And then what?"

"We'll just have to see, won't we?" he said.

"Please don't give me back to my husband, and please don't kill me," she said, hating the tremor in her voice. In her normal life, before being kidnapped, she was strong, and it would be easy to not beg for her life. She could stand here and be firm. But right now? All she could think about was the fact that this guy held that decision in his hand, and he didn't seem to care, one way or another.

"I don't know. Why not kill you though?"

"Well, for one thing, it'll mess up your car," she snapped.

He burst out laughing. "If it was mine, I might care," he said. "But, since it's stolen, I don't really give a shit."

"Ah," she said, "so you're willing to carry that on your conscience?"

"If I had one, I might care," he said callously. "But obviously I don't, so there you go."

"Right," she said, with a sigh. "It doesn't matter to you, so whatever."

"Won't you keep fighting?"

"Why would I fight?" she said quietly. "You don't care either way. It's not enough that you have the money, you want blood."

"I don't like spilling blood," he said conversationally. "I wonder if something like karma or fate is out there. I don't want to test it too much."

"Well, you must," she said quietly, "because of what you're doing."

"Ah, don't be so melodramatic," he said. "There are all kinds of reasons for me doing what I'm doing. If I can get out of killing somebody, I do."

"So, if my husband finds out that I'm alive, then what?"

"Well, then he'll come after me," the kidnapper said, "but it won't be my problem."

"How did you know I was in trouble?"

"I saw you crawl out of the back seat of a vehicle on the ferry," he said. "It's obvious you were in a panic to get away. How could I not take advantage?" And he laughed and laughed.

She froze. She'd pretended to be unconscious when her initial kidnappers had checked on her, but, realizing they hadn't secured the back door as they should have, she'd taken her chance and had escaped. She'd had no idea where she was before that, until she saw the ferry, surrounded by water. Apparently this asshole had seen her escape. "So, instead of coming to help me," she cried out, "you kidnapped me instead?"

"Well, when I see an opportunity like that," he said, "there's usually money to be made, and that's all I was particularly worried about. Saving your ass wasn't part of it. If you're lucky, it might still happen. But I wouldn't count on it."

CHAPTER 2

STILL BLINDFOLDED AND bound, her gag back in place, Stacey sank back into the trunk—the lid still popped open, so her kidnapper could stand over her—and she tried to shift her position. After the multiple blows to her head, her headache had come on hard and fast. Her throat was also parched. She was desperately in need of water. But she also knew her kidnapper was cold as ice and didn't give a shit. Who could possibly watch a woman crawl out of a car and escape and then see her as prey, instead of a victim?

She wanted to shake her head but knew that any movement would make her brains rattle, and she would cry out a little bit more. Something she was desperate to avoid. As it was, it seemed like the world was against her, and she didn't quite know why.

The one thing that struck her right now was the silence around her; it was deafening, just a weird sense of waiting—whether she was picking that up from her current kidnapper or not, she didn't know, but it was eerie. With her head covered, she couldn't see if it was light or dark out, but it felt dark; it felt cold, and it felt clammy. Was she inside this trunk in an underground parking lot? Or out in the cool air in some secluded spot? She felt a bit of a breeze, so she assumed the car was parked outside. But where? The lid to the trunk had only been opened for a few minutes, but it seemed like a chill was in the air already.

She knew the days in Canada could be hot but hadn't really expected the coolness to come down so fast afterward. Then again, for all she knew, it was a gray rainy night, and a storm was about to break. Just because she assumed that the sun had gone down didn't mean it had.

They were definitely in the northern part of Canada, and the evenings would be cool. She groaned because she was just trying to make up for the bits and pieces missing from her senses right now. The gag cutting into her cheeks and lips left a dustiness from the cloth in her mouth. As gags went, it was effective because it dried out her mouth, and she couldn't swallow. If she did manage to swallow a little bit, then she would get a layer of dust off the gag.

The blindfold was dark enough that she couldn't see through it, and it was musky enough that it gave her a headache, just to add to the rest of her headache. Her hands were tied, and she felt some sticky slipperiness to them, so she assumed her skin had been cut, and she was bleeding.

All in all, the things she discovered by tuning in to her five senses just fueled her despair. What was missing was any sound of laughter, any perception of light, any feeling of warmth or sense of security. She felt like this was the end of the road, that whatever was happening was plain old bad news. Who would do the exchange for this second ransom for her, and what did that mean for her? If the man who showed up here with the ransom was truly from her father, then she would be safe, but she was a long way from Florida, where her father lived. More than likely, her husband was involved, no matter what.

She saw Max sending somebody else out, just to make sure the job was done. That would be so typical of him. And yet she couldn't even assume that because obviously another player was involved here. And her mind still got stuck on the fact that this asshole, instead of helping her, had kidnapped her. Who gets kidnapped twice?

Why did the world hate her? What had she done wrong? That question kept playing over and over in her brain, and she had no answer, nobody to even ask. Maybe she deserved whatever she got. Sinking quickly into a fugue of depression, she almost missed it—the only sound she'd heard since they'd been here.

Then her kidnapper whispered quietly, "If you want to survive this, stay quiet."

She froze; something was obviously changing, and she didn't know what. Straining for any sounds of a vehicle, she thought she heard a footstep. A hand landed on her shoulder making her jump.

Her kidnapper squeezed her shoulder so tight that she wanted to cry out. She writhed in pain, as her kidnapper warned her again to stay quiet. Finally he released her. "What do you want?" her kidnapper called out.

"You have something for me?" a stranger asked.

"Only if you have something for me."

She didn't recognize the new voice. She strained to hear more, but, as her kidnapper took a couple steps forward, she found it harder to hear the response from the other guy.

Then suddenly her kidnapper was right against her ear and whispered, "Move and you're dead."

Then he disappeared.

She froze, too scared to do more than breathe. Even at that, she kept her breathing calm and quiet. That didn't stop her from trying to free her hands though. They had gotten so slick now from the blood that she thought she might get them free.

Closing her eyes, she focused and pulled and pulled and pulled, and finally one hand slipped out. Immediately she got the other one free, quietly pulled her knees up against her chest, and worked on untying her feet. A rope of some kind bound them but loosely. He obviously felt that she was secure and not in danger of escaping. By pulling off one of her shoes, she could slide her foot out.

With both feet free, she quickly pulled off her gag, wondering why she hadn't done that first. Then off went the blindfold, and, though it was dark out, and she had no clue where she was, she damn well wasn't staying here. She immediately climbed out of the trunk of the vehicle, found the nearest grove of trees, and raced for cover.

She moved as silently as she could but knew it wouldn't take much for anybody to catch her. In the distance, she heard two men talking, but her footsteps were light and swift, and, as soon as she made it to the trees, she slipped into the darkness of the shadows. She didn't know if either of the men had heard her—or if either would care—as long as the one got exactly what he was looking for.

KILLIAN APPROACHED THE stranger in front of him at the street corner. "Hey, can you give me a hand?"

"Depends on what you need," the man stared at him, with a hard look.

"I'm looking for this intersection," he said, holding up his phone.

"Well, if you've got it on your phone," the stranger said rudely, "you can find where to go." With that, he turned and walked away.

Killian watched and waited until he disappeared from view, even as he texted Hatch. **Found somebody very suspicious, I'm following him.**

Exchange in ten came the response.

I'll be there.

Not only would he be there but Killian also hoped that he would have a heads-up on this asshole he was following. The only reason he made contact with him and asked him for directions was to get the make of the man. Killian's instincts said there was a good chance that he was connected to the kidnapper, but it was hard to say. He waited until the man headed around the corner, then quickly followed.

When Killian reached the corner, the guy was long gone, but Killian got a tracker on him when he held up his phone. So Killian saw where he went. Pulling up the app on his phone, he leaned against the building, checking his time, and, sure enough, the guy was heading in the right direction. With that, he sent a message back to Hatch. **Following him. So far, we're both going in the right direction.**

Hatch replied, **That was easy.**

No, I don't think so. Something very strange going on here.

Yeah, you're not kidding. But these jobs are never straightforward. If they were, any standard military personnel could handle them.

"They can handle some pretty strange shit too," Killian muttered to himself, as he looked down the street.

Darkness had settled in nicely. He kept the direction finder on, as he walked toward the rendezvous point. He had his backpack on, the money inside. The bills were marked, of course, and would show up in circulation, but he had no intention of them ever making it that far. But things had a way of going south sometimes. More often than he cared to consider.

With Hatch moving in a parallel course several blocks away, the forested area was in absolute darkness at the end of town. Nothing shone, not even a car's headlights. Killian walked toward the rendezvous point, entering a park on one of its paths, and his footsteps slowed as he got within fifty feet of tracking his guy. Up ahead was a vehicle parked with the trunk open, and somebody stood thirty feet away at the side. Killian called out a quiet greeting.

The man immediately turned and took a couple steps forward.

Well, that was good. Killian walked a little closer and said, "Where's the woman?"

"Where's the money?"

"I have it," he said, dropping the backpack off his shoulder.

"Throw it my way."

"Not until I see her," he said.

In the shadows, the stranger shrugged. "Well, you'll have to come closer then."

"She's in the car. Take her out," Killian said, not giving an inch.

The guy just laughed. "She's not going anywhere."

"You only get the money if she's alive," Killian snapped.

"Well, she was, the last time I talked to her," he growled. "I don't have time for this shit. Give me the money."

"That's easy. Give me the woman."

"What are you, some smart guy?"

"A deal is a deal," he said. "One for the other."

"Sure," he snapped. "But I've got the girl, so I need you to toss the money my way."

"Not until I see proof of life."

The guy glared at him for a long moment, then turned and walked to the vehicle.

In the darkness Killian heard him muttering something like "Horse shit."

At the vehicle he swore, then turned and raced all around the vehicle, dropping to look underneath. "She's fucking gone!" he roared.

"Or she was never there to begin with," Killian replied, as he quickly picked up the backpack and raced into the shadows. Out of sight, he watched the kidnapper. The man turned and stared in the darkness, then ripped a blue streak, words that were hard to mistake.

Killian had to find the woman, before she got herself thoroughly lost out here or before the kidnapper found her. Now another man was here, closing in on the far side. Friend or foe? Killian knew that Hatch would be somewhere close as well. He quickly sent him a text. **The woman has gotten free. She's lost out here somewhere.**

He didn't know for sure that she was lost, but he would take is as a given that any woman who had gotten herself free from a kidnapper would run hell-bent in whatever direction provided by the natural spacing of the world around her. But running blindly himself wouldn't help. He scouted around the vehicle, but it was so damn dark that he couldn't see anything.

Now, if he had night goggles, that would be a different story. But it wasn't to be. He hunkered down low and listened.

The kidnapper raced through the trees, calling out to her. "Stacey, where are you? You'll die out here. It'll get too cold, and the exposure will kill you."

There wasn't a sound.

Killian continued to listen intently, when a branch snapped to his left and slid sideways. Keeping his footsteps soft and his tread gentle, he stayed in the underbrush. It had recently rained, which helped keep the dry crackling underbrush from snapping under his feet. He moved another step over and then another. He stopped and listened, his ears strained for the smallest sound. Up ahead he heard the kidnapper yelling and shouting, sounding very pissed off. If that guy got his hands on her, she would regret it.

A man stood on the outskirts and wandered ever-so-slightly around.

Killian knew this was somebody heavily involved; Killian just didn't know why. Could Max have a man on the second kidnapper? Was this the man Killian had put the tracker on? He stood up. Only by Killian's raw instincts and the man's actions had Killian's attention been attracted to him in the first place.

His actions were suspicious before, but now they were even more so. Maybe the kidnapper had a partner, and this guy was backup. In which case, maybe he was waiting farther up for the woman to climb out of this mess, and he would take her himself. Or this was just part of the second kidnapping deal.

Killian didn't know, but he had to find her first, before either one of these guys did. He had great natural nighttime vision, but he still had to see something, at least a shadow that moved. He let his eyes adjust to the darkness around him, as he surveyed the shadows, looking for anything up ahead that stuck out a little bit too far. His gaze was slowly but surely searching the darkness around him, when he heard a slight cough, behind him. And then another slight muffled tone.

He swore at that because it was loud enough that it would bring everybody in her direction. He quickly backed up until she was a little closer, and then he heard footsteps, coming in his direction. Knowing he had no time, he quickly raced around to where she was, seeing the form of her, hiding flat against a tree.

He bent down, slapped a hand across her mouth, picked her up, and, without giving her a chance to argue, shifted a good ten meters to the side.

As soon as he stopped, he whispered against her ear, "I'm here to help. I need you to stay silent." In the darkness, he saw the whites of her eyes rolling in terror. He leaned forward and whispered, "I'm part of a US Special Ops team. Stay still and quiet."

She nodded, and he released his hand on her mouth. She took a long slow deep breath and released it with her mouth open, which he hardly approved of, but it was the only way to get that air out without it becoming a harsh gasp that everybody heard.

He twisted his head. More sounds approached, coming from where he had been. He twisted a little bit more, looking around for a place to perch. He found it up just ahead, and he carried her as he made his way over ever-so-quietly and, in a sudden movement, lifted her to a branch up above. She sat perched up there, hanging on to the tree trunk, staring at him in shock. He used his fingers to tell her to circle around, so she could hug the tree trunk, as he faced the woods behind them.

He stopped then and waited, looking for anything that would tell him when the attack would come. He wasn't armed, which was something he planned to change as soon as he could. An odd sound came off to the side. He listened, not sure if this was the second man.

Then came a birdcall.

But it wasn't his, not one he knew. But it was enough that the second man nearby straightened ever-so-slightly, whispered again under his breath, but it sounded like another swear word, and then backtracked his way out. Killian didn't know what the hell was going on, but something was, and too many people were involved for him to be comfortable. He waited long enough to be sure that the two men he was aware of were backing out, but he still hadn't heard a vehicle, and he needed to know that they were done and gone.

He pulled out his phone and quickly sent Hatch a text.

Hatch responded. **I disabled the car.**

At that, Killian groaned because then he couldn't hear if they'd left or not. He waited for Hatch to add more, and, when he didn't, he asked, **See anyone?**

No sign of anyone. I think they've gone.

We need to see them go.

Killian stayed where he was for another twenty minutes, not moving, not doing anything but waiting.

Then he heard a rustle in the brush up ahead, somebody swearing in the darkness, as one of the men got up from his hiding spot and steadily moved out toward the road again. When the man got to the vehicle, the swearing increased, as he tried to start the car. He slammed the doors and fast-walked toward the center of town. And that suited Killian just fine. Checking his phone for the tracker, he noted the other man had headed back toward town as well, at least as far as the disabled car. So either the tracked guy was working in tandem with the kidnapper or he was keeping track of this second kidnapper.

At that, Hatch sent him a message. **All clear.**

Killian shifted and looked back up at the woman, still hugging the tree. In a low voice he said, "Hi, my name is Killian."

She looked down at him and whispered, "I'm Stacey."

"Got yourself in a spot of trouble, I understand."

"Double trouble actually," she said, her gaze huge. "After I escaped from the first kidnapping, a man, who should have helped me, kidnapped me instead."

At that, he stopped and stared. "What?"

She motioned toward the car. "I was on the ferry and slipped out of the back of a vehicle, away from the first kidnappers," she said. "Then this guy saw me and knocked me out. Instead of helping me, he saw an opportunity to make a buck and held me hostage himself."

"*Nice guy*," he muttered.

She whispered, "Are you alone out here?"

"No," he said. "I have a partner."

"Good," she said. "I don't know what my kidnapper might do."

"Well, somebody else is out here. That's for sure," he said. "I just don't know who they are, whose side they are on, and whether they're working together or if one is after the other."

"I would be totally okay if the latter was the case," she said.

"Well, you're safe now." He watched as she hesitated and just stared at him. "What?"

"May I see your ID?" she asked, as if grabbing her courage.

He looked at her in approval. "Good thing you asked,"

he said. "But it's hardly something I carry around with me." But, with inspiration, he held up his pointer finger, typed in Jerricho's name and number into his phone, and called him. When he answered, Killian said, "I've got you on speaker. Jerricho, I have your kidnap victim here, but I don't have any ID on me to prove who I am."

Jerricho answered and said, "Stacey, we were sent by your father."

"It's easy enough to say that," she said, her voice tremulous. "I've been to hell and back, kidnapped twice now. I am not up for a third time."

Jerricho said, "Hold on. I'll patch you through to your dad."

There was a series of *clicks*, and she looked down at Killian and asked, "Can he do that?"

"Hell yes," he said.

Another voice came on the phone, older, almost shaky. "Stacey?"

"Dad," she cried out.

"Are you okay?" He paused. "I asked these men to help because I don't have any connections anymore, and they have more than either of us could ever imagine."

"That's fine," she said. "I'm okay. I'm just trying to confirm this guy is who he says he is."

"Well, I'm not sure which one you've got there," he said, "but Jerricho can give you a description."

At that, Jerricho's voice kicked in and said, "Stacey, Killian's with you. He's an inch over six feet tall and thirty-four years old. He's a white Caucasian male, with new blond streaks in his hair, several old injuries, including some scars on the left side of his neck and the back of his hands."

At that, Killian walked a little closer, his phone flashlight on revealing his neck and raising both hands, so that she saw his scars.

"And he works for the government, the US government?" she asked.

"Yes," he said. "If you're in his hands, you're safe."

"But he's talking to somebody else. How do I know he hasn't been compromised?"

At that term, Killian's eyebrows shot up.

"He is working with Hatch," Jerricho said quietly. "He's another good man. They came to get you."

"I so want to believe you," she said, trying now to hold her voice steady. "It's just been a long and very scary trip."

"Sweetheart, you're okay now," her father said. "Let them help you."

"I hope you're right, Dad," she said. "Because the last asshole kidnapper caught me sneaking away from my initial kidnappers, and, instead of helping me," she said bitterly, "he snatched me up, knocked me out, and threw me into the trunk of his vehicle, where he tied me up and crammed a gag in my mouth."

"Jesus," her father said.

"And he had my ID from my purse, so it's not like I could hide who I was, but he contacted you, probably realizing that I had some value. Speaking of which, I need my purse from the car."

"Well, it's a good thing he did," her father said. "Because, once I knew what had happened, I could save you."

"Thanks, Dad."

Once Killian put away the phone, he looked up at her. "Are you okay?" he asked.

She took a long slow deep breath. "Yes," she said. "I think I am."

Reaching up a hand, he said, "Let me help you down."

She reached down for him, and, as soon as her fingers closed in his, he turned and said, "Just slide down onto my shoulders," which she did. Then he gently let her all the way down. "Take it easy now," he said.

"My leg," she said. "The second kidnapper, he hurt me. He did it on purpose, to keep me from running away. Said it would make me more compliant."

"The bastard." Killian faced her. "There are bastards all over this world," he said, "but not all men are bastards."

"All bastards aren't men either," she said, and she stood straighter, shaky on her one leg.

"Let's get you back to the hotel, where we can get you cleaned up. Maybe to a hospital too," he said. "It depends on how bad your leg is and how much medical attention you need."

"I don't want to go to a hospital," she said.

"Why is that?"

"Because he told me that he could find me there."

At that, Killian stopped and stared. "What? This guy who just had you?"

"Yes," she said. "So I don't know if he has access to their computer systems or if he haunts the emergency rooms or if he works there or what. He told me that I was his ticket out."

"Out of what?"

"I don't know for certain. From the way he talked, I think he meant his life in this town or something."

"That's interesting," he said. "Well, I have a tracker on another man who stood on the periphery of all this. So maybe you need to tell me all about the first kidnapping."

"I will," she said. "As soon as I can. But, right now, I

need some help for my leg."

He picked her up and carried her carefully toward the path.

"Where are we going?"

"Back to the vehicle," he said.

"I thought it wouldn't start?"

"It wouldn't," he said. "My partner disabled it, so the guy couldn't take off with you. Hopefully we can put it back together again and get you to the hotel." When she hesitated, he looked at her and said, "Do you have something against the hotel too?"

"I hope not," she said. "I'm just leery of it all."

"With good reason," he said. He slowly stepped out onto the road, and there was Hatch, standing at the car. "Does it run?" Killian asked Hatch.

"It starts," he said, "but something's not right. I wouldn't count on it going very far."

"Dang," he said. "Her leg is injured. I was hoping we could drive."

Immediately Hatch raced forward. "We can carry her between us."

"That wouldn't be much fun," she said, gasping as he put her down on her feet.

"Maybe not," he murmured, "but certainly doable."

"Is it a long way?" she asked.

"Just a few blocks." Killian looked at the car and said, "Screw it. Let me see if I can get this back into commission." He popped open the hood, and, within a few minutes, the engine turned over.

She cried out in joy.

He walked around and carefully helped her into the back seat, nodding at Hatch to drive. "Stacey, I know you probably didn't get much chance to see this last asshole, but, if you can tell us anything about him, that would help."

"I didn't get a chance to see anything," she said. "He blindfolded me almost immediately."

"That's fine. Let's not worry about it right now. We'll get you back to town and get that leg looked after."

As Killian got into the back seat with Stacey, Hatch looked at him. "Hospital?"

"Not if we can help it. The kidnapper told her that he could find her if she went to any hospital."

"Shit," he said. "Do you think it was an empty threat?"

"I don't know. It seems pretty specific. I'm sending in a request for a doctor with discretion, who will make a house call."

"Oh, good," he said. "That's better yet."

They were quiet on the drive back into town, trying to let her relax a bit. As soon as they got to the hotel, he hopped out, swung her up in his arms, and said, "We'll take you in the back entrance."

"Is that okay?" she whispered, her face turning gray.

He looked at her and frowned. "How badly hurt are you?"

"I'm not sure. I didn't think it was that bad," she said, "until I started to run through the brush, and then it really was bad. Both times I was kidnapped, I was kept with my legs and hands tied behind my back, and, after a while, everything just went numb."

"Maybe that was a gift," he said.

"I think it may have been," she gasped, as he walked in the back entrance and headed up to his room.

"The adrenaline has probably been keeping the pain at bay to some degree too," he said.

"Are you sure that a doctor will come?"

"Yes," he said. "I can guarantee that."

"How long?"

He paused in front of the door and waited while Hatch opened it. As soon as they stepped inside, he smiled. "How about right now?" he said, motioning to the man standing there, a big medical bag in front of him. Killian looked at the doctor and said, "Let's get her treated." He walked over with her and sat her down on the couch, already covered with a blanket.

She looked up at the stranger. "Who are you?"

"A doctor," he said. "One who will not talk."

"Good," she said. "Because somebody in your field is definitely talking. Otherwise there's no way my kidnapper could know where I was."

Killian watched the doctor as he quickly checked over her leg. It was very bloody, but most of it was dried. As the doctor cut off one leg of her pants, Killian knew she would need clothes and quickly sent out an order for pants, shoes, T-shirts, and a jacket, for the cold nights.

The doctor had a red swollen mark on the back of his wrist that looked like an old scratch, but it was big enough that it was still angry.

"What'd you do to your wrist?" he asked the doctor.

"Oh this?" he said. "Yeah, a bad scratch, from a dog I tried to help."

"Doesn't sound like the dog appreciated it."

The doctor laughed. "Nope, he sure didn't. But that's what happens when you help people sometimes too," he said, with a gentle smile at Stacey.

She looked even more peaked, as the doctor gently sponged the blood off her legs. "It really, really hurts," she said, trembling.

Killian walked over and sat down beside her. Grabbing her hand to divert her attention, he said, "I'm sorry." He looked at the doc. "Do you have anything for the pain?"

He nodded. "Yeah, I do. I just want to make sure that we know what the injuries are first." With the blood now sponged off, he took one look and winced. "Okay," he said. "This is worse than I thought."

CHAPTER 3

IT WAS ALL Stacey could do to sit here quietly as the doctor injected a local anesthetic all along the site of the wound. She had a huge gash on her leg. It wasn't terribly deep, but it was long and angled. So, every time she moved, skin pulled and tore a little bit more. She closed her eyes and squeezed Killian's fingers as hard as she could, as the doctor now slowly stitched his way through the layers, closing up the wound.

"I would have liked to have seen this in the hospital," he muttered to Killian.

"Well, if this guy hadn't said what he did," Killian murmured back, "we would have taken her there. We can't take a chance at this point. She's been kidnapped twice by two different factions, and we don't know what's going on. So we can't risk it a third time."

The doctor looked up sharply at that and nodded.

She just gave him a half smile, but it was so tinged in pain that more teeth showed than lips. "Are you almost done?" she gasped.

"Just about," he said in a steady voice. Finally he straightened, looked at it, and nodded. "I want to see these stitches in another ten days," he said. "And you're not to do any running, crazy jumping, or being stuffed into the back of any car trunks. Okay?" he said, teasing her.

"I'll try not to," she said.

"Now, let me have a look at those wrists."

As he worked, she relaxed a bit, leaning back ever-so-slightly. Her leg was just this burning appendage, and she didn't know where the pain started and stopped. Sure, some local anesthesia helped, but it wasn't doing enough of a job. It hurt, and it was all she could do to stay quiet.

As the doc finished up and stepped to his medical bag, Killian sat up, lifted their clenched hands, and whispered, "If you let me have my hand, I'll go put on some coffee."

She stared at him uncomprehendingly.

He lifted their hands again, so she saw.

She winced and slowly disentangled her fingers. "Did I hurt you?"

"Doesn't matter if you did," he said in a sincere voice. "You're doing just fine."

"It doesn't feel like it." She looked at him. "You're a liar," she murmured. And then she motioned toward the doctor. "If he has any pain pills …"

At that, Killian stood and walked to speak to the doctor. She only heard part of the conversation but watched as two pill bottles were handed over. And then another. She presumed that last one was an antibiotic. Killian also had a packet of gauze, bandages, ointment, and something else. She groaned as she thought about the dressing being changed on a regular basis.

As it was, all she wanted to do was take enough pain pills to knock herself out. The trouble was, she knew that all the nightmares from the last few days would continue at a subconscious level, destroying whatever bit of sleep she could possibly get.

At another knock on the door, she froze. Killian didn't

even look at the door, recognizing the distinctive knock, turning in her direction instead, with a smile. "It's Hatch. He went to get food."

She stared at him in confusion. "I didn't even know he left," she murmured.

"Don't worry about it because he's back." He walked to the door, opened it, and, sure enough, Hatch came in, carrying large bags and a tray. He looked at the doctor and asked, "Did you want to eat too, Doc?"

The doctor smiled, shook his head, and said, "Nope, I'm going home to a good home-cooked meal."

"Well, we would if we could," Hatch said, with a smile. He handed off something to the doctor, which she presumed was money to pay for the bill, but she didn't know.

She nodded at the doctor and said, "Thank you."

"No thanks needed," he said. "Guys like us have to be out there to stop things like this from happening." He waved an arm in her direction, while reloading his medical bag, then stopped. He looked at her in concern and said, "Be sure to take all the antibiotics until they are gone. And no more than two pain pills every four hours. If you need more during the night," he said, "I've given Killian a second painkiller that you can take, of a different kind. I don't want you to overdose because you are hurting."

"Oh, it's definitely hurting," she gasped.

"I know, and I'm sorry," he said. "I did give you a pain shot not very long ago, although you probably didn't even notice."

She stared at him, then looked at her arm, now throbbing a bit. "You're right. I didn't," she said. "How long before it works?"

"Hopefully soon," he said. "It shouldn't be more than

twenty minutes."

"Is it twenty minutes yet?"

He smiled. "You're almost there."

"Good," she said, the shakes quaking through her system. In an almost drugged state of mind, she watched everything happening around her. The whole thing was so surreal anyway. She'd been enjoying a nice calm day, and then all of it had been blown out of the water. She'd been on the Olympic Peninsula, then picked up and tossed into the back of a vehicle. She didn't remember anything after that, except the blow to her head.

She reached up and touched it and winced.

The doctor stopped repacking his bag and asked, "Wait. Do you have other injuries?"

She looked up at him. "I don't think so," she said. "I got hit across the face a couple times, and the original blow was to the back of my head."

Immediately his fingers worked over her head, even as he shot Killian a hard look. "You guys have to tell me these things," he said in exasperation.

"Don't blame him," she said quietly. "I haven't had a chance to even say anything."

"It's the first thing he should have asked."

"It might have been that way," she said, "but we were still in danger, and, after that, I was being very deliberate about making sure he was who he said he was. I insisted on ID and then a phone call, before I would even talk to him or get down from the tree. By the time we got to the car and then headed to town, he was focused on getting me to you."

"Well, that's a good thing," he said. "The bottom line though is, I'm not too happy with this head injury. Everything I've given you will be fine, but you stay where you are, no moving around."

"Great," she said. "If that's something I can possibly do, that'd be perfect, but I don't know if I can."

"It's not an option," he said. "You do it." He then turned to Killian. "If she has blackouts, gets dizzy, you know we have to consider a concussion."

"The worst of the blows were a few days ago," she said.

"No new blows?"

She thought about and then shrugged. "A couple but they weren't anywhere near as hard."

"Still," the doctor said, "it all compounds."

"Okay," she said, "but I should be fine now."

"You will be," he said, "because I've asked Killian here to make sure you are."

She groaned. "Haven't they done enough for me?"

"Nope, now that they've saved your life, they're responsible for it," the doc said in a laughing tone.

"That's the last thing I want," she said. "Honestly I really just want to go home."

"And we'll arrange it," Killian said, "but you're not in any shape to be traveling right now, especially not to Florida—or wherever you consider home now."

She sighed, as she looked down at her leg. "It is what it is." At that, she watched as the doctor gave her a smile, then walked out of the hotel room with Killian, and the door closed behind the two of them. She looked over at Hatch. "I heard you brought food?"

"I brought back plenty and was just about to take everything out," he said. "What would you like?"

"Some of everything," she said. "And, if Killian doesn't come back, I'll eat his share too."

Hatch burst out laughing.

She gave him a grin. "I shouldn't be hungry, but they didn't feed me much."

"Did they feed you at all?"

"Some weird shakes," she said. "They tasted awful."

"I know. I'm supposed to take protein shakes, but, to me, they all taste awful."

She nodded. "If you can get some decent things in it, like the sweeter ones, they aren't bad. But, too often, they're full of all that healthy stuff."

"And I even like healthy stuff," he said. "But, for me, I'd rather have a kale salad than have it all minced up and poured down my throat in a shake."

"Well, it wasn't green. It wasn't anything like that," she said. "It had a chalky, powdery taste. I figured it was probably laced with drugs, to keep me more compliant."

"Were you difficult?"

She gave him a flat stare. "As bad as I could be, as often as I could pull it off. Hence all the blows to my head."

"Got it," he said. "Remember. Resistance should be doled out carefully. Then it's actually effective."

"Oh, so not when you're in a blind panic?"

"Well, that too," he said. "Sometimes it's just hard not to."

"And sometimes," she said, "it's sheer frustration, and you need the relief, so you can focus on another plan for the next time."

"Wow, I get that too," he murmured. "Good for you, for keeping some resistance going."

"I guess it's hard, isn't it?"

"A lot of people struggle with it," he murmured.

She looked at the bags on the table. "Did you unpack them all?"

"I did," he said as he lifted the empty bags, so she saw.

"What are my choices?"

"It's all Italian," he said.

"Is there lasagna?" she asked hopefully.

He nodded and pulled off a tinfoil lid from one square-shaped package. "Can you eat this much?"

She nodded.

He brought it over on a plate, with a towel underneath it to protect her from the heat. He gave her a fork. "If you need me to cut it, let me know."

"I hope not," she said, shifting gingerly and only wincing slightly as she put herself into a more upright position to hold the food closer to her. He quickly scooped up pillows and placed them on her lap, so she could rest the lasagna on top. Then he tucked a towel around her as a bib.

She snorted at that. "These clothes are so history anyway. What I wouldn't give for fresh clothes."

At that, the door opened, and Killian walked back in. He smiled when he saw her sitting up with food. "Did I just hear you ask for clothing?"

"Absolutely," she said. "If you guys can produce a meal like this right now when I'm starving, clothing should be easy for you." He laughed and held up the bag he carried. She stared at it, back to him, and said, "What's that?"

"The clothes I ordered for you."

She stared at him in shock. "Seriously?"

"Yeah," he said. "But are you sure you want to get fresh clothes on now, when you'll make a mess of it right away?" And he pointed to her leg.

She winced and said, "That's not fair."

"No, but just hold on to the thought that pretty soon you'll get into something clean."

"Damn," she said, staring down at her leg. "We're supposed to put a dressing on it, aren't we?"

"We will after we eat," he said.

"Meaning?"

"Let's let the painkillers have some time to kick in a little more."

"Okay," she said. "I can get behind that."

"I'm sure you can," he said, with a smile. Then he walked over, scooped up a container for himself, and said, "I didn't know a pasta joint was around here."

Between bites, she said, "It's really good too."

"Or you're just really hungry," he teased.

"I was just telling Hatch that they didn't give me very much in the way of sustenance," she said.

"Okay," Killian began. "This is as good a time as ever. Tell us exactly what happened, from the beginning."

She shrugged and said, "I left my husband's home in Texas and drove as far away from him as I could, crossing the Canadian border. I was at the Olympic Peninsula, just walking down the street. I turned the corner and was headed down a side street, looking for a small bookstore. Two men got out of a vehicle and asked me for directions. I told them that I didn't really know where I was myself, so I wouldn't be any help. Then I was hurled to the side of a vehicle, and suddenly I was inside it. They hopped in, closed the door, and, next thing I knew, I blacked out. I think they put something over my head and knocked me out. I'm not sure. It just all happened so fast that I really don't know exactly."

"And that's fine," Killian said in a soothing voice. "When did you wake up again?"

"I woke up in a van a while later. I'd been gagged, tied up, my head covered. I think they thought it would act as a blindfold as well, but I saw through it a little bit. Enough to know there were two men, and I heard a conversation that I thought involved Max—my husband, we're separated—so, in a way, that made an ugly kind of sense."

"So the little bit that we've heard about Max," Hatch said, "is that your soon-to-be ex is a nasty piece of work, and, when you decided to leave the marriage, you took something of his along with you?"

"Maybe," she said. "Anyway I tried to escape from my kidnappers at that point in time, but I couldn't really see a whole lot. While they were talking, I got the rear door kicked open with my feet on a lever and managed to hop out. One of the ties came loose on my feet, and I started to run. I heard them coming up behind me and knew I wouldn't get far, but I was hoping that someone would see me. With my hands still tied and that damn hood on, not being able to see that well, I was quickly picked up, hauled back to the van, and knocked out again.

"I don't know what happened after that. But, when I woke up, my head was killing me. I was alone with one of the men, and he told me that it was my fault and that I would get more of a beating each time I tried to escape again."

Hatch shook his head, muttering.

Killian said, "Carry on. This is hard for me to hear, so I know it must be worse for you to tell. But we need to know all that you can share."

She shrugged. "I don't even know how long I was with them. I'm sure they drugged me. I would wake up, forced to drink this weird shake, and I'd sleep again. Then I'd wake up and get another one and sleep. At one point, I upchucked after one of the drinks, and I didn't end up falling back asleep again. I felt the vehicle moving and realized I was in the back seat of a big transport rig. We were stopped in a line for a long time. Then we drove over some metal-sounding grates before parking. The two men talked in low tones, but one turned to check on me, saying, *She's still out. Let's lock her in and go stretch our legs.* They got out, slammed the doors, and walked away.

"I finally got my hands around my feet and in front of me again. I reached for the latch with my bound hands. After a few minutes, I managed to get it open, and I slipped out the side of the van but fell to the ground. I pushed the bag off my eyes and pulled down the gag, then I started working on the ropes. I hadn't been tied up too securely because I was always drugged, and, as soon as I managed to untie my hands and feet, I quickly closed the door to the rig, and I slipped through the vehicles. I was on a ferry.

"What I didn't realize at the time was that somebody had seen it all and had essentially watched me save myself," she said bitterly. "As I worked my way through the vehicles, he stepped up and asked me if I was okay. I was taken in by his kind demeanor. I didn't even really get a look at him, and then, next thing I knew, he'd clipped me hard on the side of the head, and I was out. When I woke up, I was bound again."

"Wow," Hatch said. "I wonder if that was just a fluke or if he'd followed you."

"I don't know," she said, "but it's shitty either way. He said he saw me escaping and grabbed me himself."

"We also have to consider," Killian added, "that he might have been the other partner in the initial kidnapping. A scenario where he knew about you and decided to set up a chance for him to make more money for himself."

She stared at him. "Wow, I didn't even think of that," she said. "Maybe?"

"Did his voice sound familiar at all?"

"I honestly don't remember," she said. "At the beginning, the voices of the first kidnappers were hard to hear because they were muffled by the bag or whatever was over my head. And this second guy had some sort of band around my eyes, tight on my head. It was wrapped around my ears too, so it was hard to hear anything clearly. So, for all I know, it could have been one of the first two guys. I have no idea. There wasn't enough difference in what I heard of their voices to know for certain. The second kidnapper did say he'd sold me twice." And she explained how one buyer wanted proof of life and the other wanted him to take her life.

Killian nodded as he walked over and sat down beside her. "How are you feeling now?"

She looked at the bowl of lasagna that she'd polished off two-thirds of. "I really wanted all of this," she said, "but I don't think I can finish it."

"Then don't," he murmured. "Just take it a little bit easy on your stomach."

"Right," she said, as she handed it to him. "Can I just sleep here then?"

"You can, but there's a bed for you here."

She looked over at him. "But that means moving."

"Your bladder will have to be emptied at some point anyway," he said.

She glared at him. "Now why would you even remind me of that?" she said. "That'll just hurt."

"It might," he said, with a big grin. "But you're fit and strong, and you've done incredibly courageous things. So don't worry about it. You'll make it through."

"Says you," she said, with a grumbling tone. "I don't feel like I've been courageous at all."

"Did you fight your kidnappers every time?"

"As often as I could. I got smacked more times than I care to remember," she said slowly, rotating her jaw. "After a while, your face just starts feeling like hamburger."

"Well, I'd say it looks like it too, but that might freak you out," he murmured.

She glared at him.

He grinned. "It's a little swollen, but it's not too bad."

She gently touched her face and then nodded. "It feels puffy."

"It is."

⚓

KILLIAN WATCHED AS Stacey sat here, as long as she could. And then he stood, held out his hand, and said, "Let me give you a hand up." Using his arm, she pulled herself upright, and he noted the color immediately faded from her skin. "I'll help you walk to the bathroom."

"I walked just fine before," she protested. "Why is it so hard now?"

"Well, for one, now you mentally know you're injured," he murmured. "And, for two, you've got stitches in your leg. So, although it's frozen with painkillers, it's swollen and injured. Your body knows that it has a chance to heal and doesn't want you on it, so it'll scream to make you get off that leg. For three, you don't have the adrenaline rush of trying to escape pumping you up."

"Great," she said. "So now even my body is trying to

hold me captive."

"But this time, it's for your own good," he said. At the bathroom door, he looked at her and said, "Will you be okay?"

"I'll be okay," she said and shut the door firmly in his face.

He chuckled.

Hatch looked at him and said, "Better watch it."

"Why?"

"Sparks."

"No, that's everybody else, not me," he said, with a shrug. "I've never been the one who would get picked in a basketball game and certainly not have the popular girl."

"Maybe not," he said. "Bu you've got to admit, she's an interesting character."

"*Very*," he said. "Cute too."

From the other side of the bathroom door, she yelled, "I'm right here, you know. I might be injured, but I'm not deaf."

"That's fine," he said. "It's not like I'll lie about it. You are cute."

She snorted. "Like hell. I'm cranky. I'm miserable. I look like shit, and I don't like being lied to."

"I'm not lying," he said.

The door opened suddenly, and she glared at him. "No way anybody can look at this face right now and say I'm cute."

He leaned forward and said, "You're cute."

She glared at him and pugnaciously stuck her chin out and said, "Am not."

"Are too."

"Am not."

"Are too."

At that, Hatch burst out laughing. "Oh, man," he said, "I wish I had this on tape."

On cue, both of them turned to glare at him as one.

At that, Killian asked, "Why? So you could send it to the rest of our team?"

"I should," he said. "Or maybe just to her father."

"Don't do that," she said. "He's been bugging me to get into a permanent relationship ever since I filed for divorce."

"Well, you probably figured that wouldn't be a good idea, considering how you feel about your husband."

"But my father loved my husband," she said. "That's why I had to bring him proof of what an asshat Max really is."

Still smirking, Hatch turned and buried his face in his dinner.

Killian looked back at her and said, "Honestly, nothing in that bruising and puffiness hides your beauty."

She shook her head and said, "You're being ridiculous." But her voice sounded more pleased than anything.

He smiled and asked, "Are you done in here? Can I help you back to your couch?"

"Since I'm up and all, I was hoping that maybe I could go to a bed?"

"Absolutely you can," he said. "Pajamas are in that bag, if you want."

She looked at him and said, "How about a nightie instead?"

"Why don't we take a look," he said. "And then we can figure out what else you might still need."

"I don't need anything," she said. "I'm just really tired, and, with my leg injury, I don't want to put on pants."

"Wait here." He brought the bag to her, and together they sorted through three sets of clothes, an oversize T-shirt, and weird shorts. He held them up and shrugged and said, "I honestly don't know about these."

She smiled and said, "Sleeper shorts. They're perfect." She grabbed the bag of clothes and shut the bathroom door in his face again.

"I could help you, you know?" he said through the door.

"Thanks anyway. I'll be just fine."

He waited, a big grin on his face, until he saw Hatch staring at him, with a smirk on his. Immediately Killian dropped the smile and said, "Don't even go there."

"Oh, I've already gone there," he said. "Gone there and back a few times."

"I wouldn't think about it at all. You don't know anything."

"Nope, I don't," he said. "But, at the same time, I'm pretty happy with what I see."

Killian groaned and said, "Just forget it." When she opened the door, he looked at her and said, "Okay, I can see how that works."

She smiled. "This should be good, for nighttime anyway."

"Okay, so let's get you to the bed, so I can dress the wound."

She winced. "Is that really necessary?"

He nodded. "Absolutely. We should have done it earlier, but the doc wanted it to dry and breathe a bit. Now that it's dry, and you're more or less as numb as you'll be, we'll bandage it up. That way, when you roll over in the night, you won't catch those stitches in the bedding or the mattress and shriek from the pain."

"That sounds horrible already," she said, staring at him.

"Exactly, so let's get you to the bed."

She hobbled to the bed, taking her time, and he let her. After her kidnapping ordeal, it was important for her to feel as independent as possible, and, when she finally got to the edge of the bed, she sank down heavily. "Okay, now I don't feel so good," she murmured.

"A little too much independence?"

"I don't know, maybe just a little too much everything," she said. She slowly flopped onto her back and lifted both legs onto the bed, until she was stretched out.

"You should've let me take the bedding off first." She groaned and then sat back up and slid off the bed. He pulled the bedding back, and she laid back down again. He brought over the bag of medical supplies that the doctor had left him and quickly put on clean gauze and wrapped the large wound, covering all the stitches on her leg. "Maybe that'll help," he said, as he flipped a sheet over the top of her.

"Well, at least that's not hurting anyway," she said. Rolling over onto her good leg, she pulled the pillow underneath her head, yawned, and said, "I think I'm ready to sleep."

"You need your pain pills and an antibiotic yet," he said. "Let me get some water." He stepped into the bathroom, filled a glass of water, and came out with the pain pill bottle and shook out two, then added the antibiotic. He handed them to her, as she shifted up onto her elbow, popped them into her mouth, and drank down the glass of water.

"That's it, for me," she said, pulling the sheet up a little higher.

"Do you want a blanket too?"

She shook her head. "Not at this point," she said. "I'll try it with just the sheet. It's pretty warm in here."

"It'll get colder," he said. "But that's up to you."

"Maybe in a bit," she said. "If I can fall asleep like this, it's all good." With that, she drifted off.

He cleaned up his mess and put the trash in the bathroom garbage, then walked back to the little kitchenette area, where he wasn't surprised to see Hatch still eating. "Still hungry?"

"A lot of work done today, and I haven't had a ton of food."

"Now you sound like her," he said.

"It is what it is."

"So you say," he said. "We need to stand watch tonight."

"Agreed. Way too much we don't know yet," Hatch said. "I'm still eating. You go crash."

"You sure?"

"Absolutely," he said.

With that, Killian dropped onto the second bed, and closed his eyes. "Wake me if there's anything."

"I will," he said. "Do you need to check in?"

"No checking in is required on this job. I can if I want to, but—"

"Maybe there's information."

"So check in then," Killian said.

"You don't mind?"

"Hell no," he replied. "You're supposed to be assisting me anyway."

"Is that what I'm supposed to be doing?" Hatch said, with a note of humor.

"Yeah."

"What about the guy you're tracking?" Hatch asked.

At that, Killian sat back up. "Yeah, I don't know what's with that guy."

"Do you have him still in your tracker?"

He shook his head. "No, it stopped back there at the getaway car."

"Like when we picked her up?"

"By the time we got to the car, it had already stopped."

"Interesting. Sounds like he found the tracker and destroyed it," he said. "Too bad we don't have a clue where he went."

"I want to know what the hell he was doing," Killian said. "When you think about it, he had absolutely no reason to be there at all."

"Unless he was connected somehow, and that's possible. If that's the case, then we need to figure out exactly what we'll do about it."

"The only thing we can do," he said, "is try to get a rundown on him. I already asked for the camera feeds to take a look for facial recognition hits." Just then his phone buzzed. "What do you want to bet that's Jerricho now." He snatched his cell off the night table. After checking, he got up, walked back to the kitchen table, brought out his laptop, and signed into the secure chat. **Any news?**

Nothing popped on facial recognition. Do you have any other details?

No, his voice was a little on the raspy side, but I'm not sure if that was natural or deliberate. I couldn't see his features very well at all.

Distorted?

He thought about it and shrugged. **It's possible. He had a cap pulled down, a beard, and wore a big hoodie, ruffled up around the neck.**

So, not a whole lot to see, like cheekbones or sunken eyes, because of the cap.

Right. And the tracker isn't working anymore, so it's

been removed, or it's broken, or he's out of range.

All three are possible, right?

Yeah, I don't even know if he was anything other than an innocent bystander. I didn't like his actions, and I went on instinct, and he was an ass when I asked for directions. The fact that he then showed up close to where we found her makes me doubly suspicious.

Could be he followed you.

No, he was ahead of me.

Well, stay alert, Jerricho said. **How's she doing?**

I'm sure you've already talked to the doctor by now. She just fell asleep, and that's exactly what she needs right now, a good rest.

Yeah, and he sent me a picture of the leg, and I'm glad for that, so at least we have some idea of what we're looking at. Hopefully she'll heal enough to get moving soon.

She'll be fine in another day or so, Killian wrote. **It's just, after her entire experience, she probably needs a day or two to just chill and relax. It won't hurt her in the least.**

Easy for you to say. She might have a different answer.

CHAPTER 4

STILL MOSTLY ASLEEP, Stacey shifted, then snapped awake, crying out in pain.

Almost immediately a hand gently landed on her shoulder, and a calm voice said, "You're okay. Just relax."

"It hurts," she whispered.

"That's because it's time for your pain pills."

A soft light turned on beside her, and she saw Killian's face above her. Instantly the memories came rushing back. "Oh, God," she said. "I was hoping that was all just a bad nightmare."

"Well, the good news is," he said, with a note of humor, "that the nightmare is over, and you have been rescued."

"Right," she said, giving her face a scrub. She sat up and cried out again. "Jesus, that hurts." She stared down at her leg.

"Well, that's a lot of stitches, and it went untreated for several days, so the doc had to do quite a bit of trimming to get a clean and stable place to start from. The wound's a bit on the rough side, but again, things are looking up because it's been treated, and you'll be fine."

"I remember that," she said, with a slow nod, "though I don't remember much else right now. My head's kind of fuzzy."

"That could be a side effect of the medication too," he

said.

He picked up two pill bottles, while she watched, and he handed three pills to her. With the glass of water on the night table she popped them back, grimacing as she swallowed them. "My throat is sore," she said, then had some more water, sipping it carefully.

"That's from a lack of water for a while," he said. "The membranes dry out and get raspy."

She nodded. "I was hoping when I woke up that I'd feel better, not worse."

"Reality has to set in. Your body has been through a trauma, and it has to heal. The human body is amazing, and, now that it has a chance, it will focus on healing. But the side effect of that is a very rough ride for you for a few days."

She threw back the sheet, frowned at the sight of the blood on top of the bandage, and said, "Does that need to be rebandaged?"

He looked at it and nodded. "Yep, it sure does."

"Let me go pee first," she said. "I think that's what woke me up."

"As a kid, my bladder used to give me really terrible nightmares," he said, "in order to make me wake up and not wet the bed."

"Yeah, I think mine is doing the same," she said. "And that's not a nightmare I want to be reminded of anytime soon."

"Of course not."

He helped her to her feet, and she hobbled to the bathroom, using the wall for support every step of the way. When she got there, she closed the door and used the facilities. By the time she got back up again, she was shaking. She felt a sheen of sweat on her back, neck, and face. She opened the door to let him in, and he motioned her toward the toilet.

"Go ahead and sit back down and let's get that leg taken care of."

With her bad leg stretched out in front of her, she sat gingerly and hung on to the side of the bowl, while he removed the bandage. Parts of it were sticking, so he ran a washcloth under the hot water and gently applied it to the gauze, softening the dried blood. With the bandage off and the light on, they both took a critical look at it.

She shrugged. "It doesn't look that bad."

"No, the doc did a great job sewing that up. I think maybe, while you were sleeping, you disturbed it."

"*Great*," she said. "It's not like that's something I can prevent."

"No, you can't. But let's redo the dressing." He took the washcloth and gently sponged off the injury, taking away as much dried blood as he could. When it was clean and dry, he bandaged it up again. By that time, she was weak, and her energy level had completely bottomed out. She felt the shakiness inside once again.

He helped her back to the bed, covered her up again, and said, "Just sleep."

"If I can," she whispered. "I would love to be knocked out right now."

"Well, you might be soon," he said. "The drugs are pretty powerful, considering what you've been through."

She nodded and closed her eyes, but she trembled even more.

With a muffled exclamation, he sat down beside her and pulled her into his arms.

"What'll that do?" she asked, as her teeth chattered.

"Well, added body heat for one," he said. "But the shivering? It's not because you're cold. … It's shock."

"If you say so," she said, trying to burrow in deeper.

He grabbed the blanket at the bottom of the bed, pulled it up over her, and just held Stacey close. It took a few minutes for the tremors to slow down.

She yawned several times, feeling the furnace of his body heat around her. "I shouldn't be cold," she said. "There's enough heat in this hotel room to keep me comfortable."

"Back to you're injured, remember?" he murmured, gently rubbing her shoulders.

She let out one heavy sigh and then another one, feeling some of the stress and the tension drop away again, as the drugs took over. When she woke up the second time, she was alone. She rolled over onto her back, gingerly feeling her leg move, stiff and almost unfamiliar. But the pain wasn't screaming at her. She lay here for a long moment, staring up at the ceiling, trying to orient herself to where she was and to what had happened.

Letting her head drop to the side, she saw Hatch sleeping soundly in the next bed and Killian sitting at the kitchen table.

He looked at her, frowned, and walked to her bed. "It's still really early," he whispered. "It's just going on six now."

She nodded. "I've always been an early riser," she said. "So six is pretty normal."

"I was hoping you'd sleep quite a bit later," he said, "and give your body that extra chance to heal."

"Well, my body has been waking up early for a very long time," she said. "So we could hope, but I don't think we'll have much luck with that."

He asked, "Do you need a pain pill?"

"It's not bad at the moment," she said cautiously. "But,

if I move, I'm not sure. Depends on the bladder."

"Let me know how that goes and if you want to try to sleep."

She sat up in bed, scooting backward, and, when she sat next to the headboard, she sighed and nodded. "Definitely need a trip to the bathroom." She got up and walked over slowly, happy that her leg was moving somewhat, but it was surprisingly stiff. "I wasn't expecting the stiffness," she murmured, when she came back out.

"It's the injury," he said. "Everything stiffens up."

She nodded and made her way back to the bed and sat on the edge. "I'm not sure I can sleep anymore," she confessed.

"You want to come over here and sit down?"

"Maybe," she murmured. She made her way around the sleeping Hatch and sat on the kitchen chair across from Killian. She took a long slow deep breath and said, "Well, that wasn't too-too bad."

"Doesn't matter," he said. "You're still heading for your pain pill and the antibiotic."

She winced. "I really don't like taking drugs."

"If you want to skip a pain pill, okay. But here's the thing," he said. "There are times to be worried about medications and times not to. With a gash the size of that wound on your leg—and it's still oozing blood—we want to make sure there's no infection, so we can get you moving toward home. So don't miss any of the antibiotics."

"Well, that's guaranteed to make me behave," she said. "I just want to go home."

"And we'll get you there," he said, "but not until you're well enough to travel."

"This isn't that bad."

"No, but we've got to take care of it, or it could get bad in a hurry," he said. He reached for his phone and texted something, while she watched.

"What was that all about?"

He looked up, smiled, and said, "I thought you might like some coffee."

Her gaze widened. "I would absolutely love a coffee," she said. "And a shower."

"Nope on the shower," he said. "Unless you're okay with me coming in and helping."

"It would almost be worth it," she said, with a grimace. "I feel pretty rough."

"You might," he said, "but you're not capable of standing that long, and the last thing we need is for you to slip and fall and reinjure yourself. You'll get very tired while you're in there, and there's no seat in that shower," he said, his gaze assessing. "I'm all for helping you, if you want to give it a shot, but no modesty allowed."

She snorted at that. "I hear you. Maybe a little bit later," she said. "I'm already not feeling all that great."

"Exactly. I figure you'll manage a single cup of coffee, and then you'll probably crash again."

She gave him a lopsided smile. "I'm not sure that's a bad thing at the moment. And I'll only manage that coffee if it comes pretty quick."

Just then came a series of raps on the door.

She froze, but he seemed completely unconcerned. "I gather that's the coffee?" she asked hopefully.

"Should be." He opened the door and proceeded to pull the trolley inside.

"Wow," she said. "I didn't think this hotel would give this kind of service."

"It doesn't," he said, with a bright grin, "but we tend to arrange for over-and-above service, as we need it."

"Nice deal if you can get it," she murmured.

He smiled, as he pushed the cart toward her. "Do we want to wake up Hatch?"

"No. It's almost time for him to wake up anyway," he said. "But he's lacking on sleep, so I wanted to give him a little longer."

She smiled and nodded. "I guess, in your business, it's important to catch sleep when you can, isn't it?"

"Not only is it important to catch sleep," he said, "but you just never really know when you'll need that energy boost that comes from being well rested."

"I can imagine," she said. "I know when I was panicked, I had lots of energy. I wasn't expecting that either, but I didn't really think about it at the time."

"When you panic, you don't think—that's the thing. Your body just reacts, and it pounds out whatever you need of it, as long as it can, and then you hit the end of the wall, where it can't do any more," he said. He lifted the coffeepot and poured her a cup. Then he nudged the cream and sugar toward her.

She shook her head. "Just black for me, please."

He nodded and filled his own cup.

When he lifted the lid off another platter, she smiled. "Cinnamon buns, at this hour?"

"Hey, it's morning," he said. "I don't know what you want for breakfast, but chances are you'll do better with more frequent small meals for a little bit yet. This will give you something to keep you going."

"Never a wrong time for a cinnamon bun," she said, with a smile. "Right?"

"They are one of my favorites," he said. "So I tend to order them when I'm out." He smiled and served her one.

She sat here quietly, working her way through the cinnamon bun and coffee. When she was done, she looked at her plate and then at him. "I thought I could last longer," she said, "but I'm really tired again." She used the table to help her stand and then slowly made her way back to the bed. By the time she dropped back down into bed, she felt a sense of relief at just being able to relax into the bedding.

As she watched, he got up, came around, and lifted her legs, then gently pulled the bedding out from under her and covered her up again. "Nap if you can," he said.

She smiled, nodded, and said, "I'll try."

And she closed her eyes.

KILLIAN WASN'T SURPRISED Stacey was so tired. As soon as she drifted off, it was almost like a switch went on, and Hatch rolled over and looked at him, wide awake. "What time is it?"

"Almost seven," he said.

"Wow. And it's been peaceful?"

"It's been peaceful," he said, with a nod.

Hatch took one look at the coffee service and frowned.

"It's still hot. Don't worry," Killian said.

Hatch hopped up and went to the bathroom. When he came back out, he poured himself a cup of coffee and snagged a cinnamon bun. "How long has she been out?" He motioned toward her bed.

"She went back down just before you got up," he said. "She's doing better. We cleaned the wound earlier. She's …

She's holding up, but it'll be a little bit before she's well enough to travel."

"Well, even that leg alone will be hard to mobilize in a plane. And having to sit with her knees bent the whole time will hurt like hell."

"And that's why we need her to gain a bit more strength," he said. "Two days would make a big difference. Plus we can watch for infection."

"Any information?"

"Nothing yet. I'm still racking my brain about the guy I put the tracker on."

"What's bugging you the most about him?"

"Not quite sure. His actions. His … vibe. Whatever it is just sits in the back of my brain, driving me crazy. I know that he had covered most of his face on purpose, and that alone raises my suspicions. At the same time, I just need more information, so we can find out who he is."

"And what about the second guy who kidnapped her? He's the one we need to really track down and to make sure he doesn't come after her again."

"I know," he said. "I've asked for the cameras off the ferries in the area. They have them for the terminals only. There's talk of upgrading to all the car decks on the individual ferries but it hasn't happened yet."

"That's a good idea, too bad they haven't done it already," Hatch said.

"She's assuming it's her husband, but she didn't see him at any kidnapping event or hear him," Killian said, with a frown. "He would have hired someone. And that's troublesome too. We can't know for sure it was her husband just yet. Right now I feel like, if we take her back to her dad, we're just returning her to the same dangerous scenario."

"That wouldn't be good," Hatch said. "So we better nip this in the bud right now, while she's injured and can't travel, and then, when we finally get her home again, she'll be safe."

"That's my line of thinking, but we have two threads to tug. One from the original kidnapping, and one from the asshole who took advantage of the pickle she was in."

"I can't even imagine doing that," Hatch said, looking up at him. "That's like, you know, finding an injured puppy in the woods and, instead of helping it, just hurting it some more."

"People are assholes. We know that," Killian said quietly.

"Life is already too damn hard for any of this crap."

"I'll start with a full investigation into her husband," Killian said. "Even she suspects him of the first crime."

"And the husbands always make excellent targets," Hatch said.

From the bed, Stacey corrected the men. "My ex… he may not have signed the papers yet but we are definitely no longer together, okay?"

Killian looked at her and asked, "How long were you married?"

"Eighteen months," she said quietly, "and we were apart for a large amount of that time due to his travels. That was the only reason it lasted as long as it did."

"Why the divorce?"

"He's a sadist," she said flatly. "He likes to see other people suffer. It starts with a little emotional abuse, a little mental abuse, and then it evolves into the physical abuse."

Both men glared at her. "Did he beat you?"

She shrugged. "You know how it begins. A tough slap, a

twisted wrist here, a shoulder squeeze that's way too hard," she said. "Somehow a sudden fall down a short flight of stairs. It was all the little things, until he got me accustomed to that. And then it built up. The slightly twisted wrist became a full-on sprain. The trip down a few stairs became a fall down eight or ten. The squeeze on the shoulder became a punch. The slap across the face became an uppercut to the jaw," she said, glaring right back at them.

"I'm surprised you lasted that long."

"I didn't last very long after the last smack in the face," she said. "It was easy enough to excuse away all the rest. But that time, he told me that he would teach me a lesson I'd never forget."

"Of course," Hatch said. "That's how bullies always act."

"Well, I couldn't stand for it anymore. Up until then, I worried about my father's reaction to this abuse, as Dad was a huge fan of Max."

"How much interaction did your father have with him though?"

"Not enough," she said. She slowly sat up, shuddering at the pain.

Immediately Killian walked over and said, "Just stay in bed. You have no place to go, nothing to do, just relax."

She looked at him and then slowly sank back down again. "Just talking about that man," she said, "gets my back up."

"Then we don't need to talk about him," he said. "I'll do a full investigation into where he was then and what he's doing right now. I'm wondering just what we'll find, if he has an alibi for the time frame when you were grabbed. You seem pretty sure he was responsible for the kidnapping one way or another."

"He would have hired somebody," she said, with a wave of her hand. "He's a well-respected Wall Street investor. He has his own company. Everybody looks up to him. He's that perfect suave male on the outside, but something wrong to the core is on the inside, and, no matter how close to him you are, you don't see it until you're right there, getting punched in the face."

"Well, we'll find it, if anything's there," he said.

"I hope you find something," she said, dropping her head back onto the pillow.

He watched as she stared up at the ceiling, her hard face slowly turning vulnerable, almost ready to weep. He walked to the bed and reached down and grabbed her fingers and squeezed. "How about a fresh pot of coffee?"

She looked over at him. "Sure. And maybe some real food."

"What? That cinnamon bun didn't hold you?" he said in a joking manner. He walked back to the table where Hatch was working, snatched up his phone, and sent off a couple messages.

"I am feeling better though," she said. "But it's enough to make anybody sick to hear you talking about my ex."

"I need his full name," Hatch said, "the company name, and anything else you know."

She immediately said, "Max Edgewater. His company is Fulcrum Enterprises, and, when you're ready, I'll give you his social security number too." With his nod, she gave that to them.

"Well, that's helpful," he said, after typing it into his laptop.

"Not really. It'll only give you the surface stuff," she said. "If you can get into my old house, Max's home in Texas, that safe in his office would have a lot more interesting things in it."

"What is it you think he was doing?"

"I have no idea," she said, "but he certainly was busy with investments. Were they illegal? I have no way of knowing because it's not my area of expertise."

"When you split, did you get half?"

"Are you kidding?" she said, with a broken laugh. "Nobody gets half. He gets it all, or there is nothing."

"Did you have anything going in?"

"I had a small savings account and my vehicle," she said. "I ended up with my vehicle, and that was it."

"What happened to your savings account?"

"Oh, he invested it under my name," she said in a wry tone. "Only I found nothing in my name at the end of the day. So, when I walked, it was all his."

"*Nice*," he said. "You really, … ah, … found a winner, huh?"

"I think only losers are out there."

"Anything else you can tell us, businesswise?"

"No," she said. Then she stopped and added, "He has a good friend, James Dean."

"What's he like?"

"Almost as bad, maybe worse. They should be brothers," she said bitterly. "He's the type of guy who would sell his own mother into the sex slave market." She gave Killian and Hatch a little bit more information on Dean, but it wasn't a whole lot.

"Good enough," Hatch said. "I've got enough to work with."

"Good," she said. "If you find something criminal, I wouldn't be at all upset if you nailed their asses to the wall."

"Including this James Dean person?"

"He's just as bad as Max is," she murmured. She shook herself, as if shaking off an ugly memory.

"Did he ever hit you?"

"James? No. Although once, after Max hit me, James told me that it was my fault."

At that, both Hatch and Killian exchanged hard looks. "Sounds like they just egg each other on then," Killian said. "It's a good thing you're out of that situation."

"It is. I also had to walk away with nothing," she said. "It was either that, or I wouldn't walk away."

"You really think he'd have killed you?"

"No, not necessarily, but I don't think breaking both legs and paralyzing me would have been out of the question."

"And yet I understand from your father that you took something as … as insurance of a sort?"

"Because I didn't trust that Max would let me walk away," she said quietly.

"But you realize that, by taking something, you may have started him on this path?"

"Quite possibly, yes," she said. "It was a risk I had to take."

"And you told Max about it?"

"Only after he heard it from my father."

"What?"

She looked over and nodded. "You have to understand. My father is a gentleman—and a southern gentleman at that. He had me late in life, so he's the age of some of my friends' grandfathers. A handshake is all that's required to move millions of dollars, and, when he says something, he means it. Plus, in his world, men don't punch women. He couldn't conceive of Max doing such a thing."

"Ah, I get it, and he projected his personality and mindset on your husband, not seeing the real Max."

"Yes, so initially Dad was disappointed in my behavior," she said, shifting in the bed, setting the pillows up behind her and getting more comfortable. "He blamed me."

"For getting hit?" Killian's voice rose, as he stared at her.

"Worse than that, I think he didn't believe me. I didn't show him the medical records, and I certainly didn't go to him when I got hurt," she said, staring at Killian. "But, when I told him that I had taken some insurance, he felt embarrassed that I would do such a thing."

"Good Lord," Hatch said, sitting back in his chair. "He really wasn't there for you, was he?"

"No, and he definitely regrets that now, no doubt."

"But does he truly believe that your ex would do this?"

"I'm not sure that he does. For all I know, he could still be thinking that I'm making it up or hoping that I'm wrong. But I'm not wrong. Dad is."

Killian nodded. "And that abhorrent behavior is very hard for anybody with ethics to accept. But, in something like this, where it was his daughter at risk—*ugh*."

"Exactly," she said, leaning back and closing her eyes. "And some of the insurance I told him about made him question it again."

"What kind of insurance are we talking about?"

She looked at Killian. "I think Max is … dealing, dealing weapons out of Texas."

Both men stared at her, now sitting on the bed opposite hers.

"Do you have anything to back that up?" he asked. "Because that's not just let-me-walk-out-of-house-safely insurance, Stacey. That's we'll-shoot-you-dead-and-ask-questions-later kind of insurance."

"I know that now," she said. "But I didn't know what I had, until I left."

"You need to explain this a little bit better."

"Okay. So, on my final day there, I was home alone, packing up the last of my things. Max wasn't there, and I went through his office, trying to figure out where my savings money was," she said. "He told me that I would never get it, that I'd never find it again because he'd moved it, and it was no longer under my name, reminding me what a fool I was for having signed it away with his paperwork." With that, she added, "He didn't have to tell me that of course. I was a fool and worse. I trusted my husband, and, well, you can see where that got me."

"You lived and learned," Hatch said. "Now get back to the weapons."

"When I was in his office, I found notes on a notepad—about AK-47s, plus several different variations of handguns, a bunch of numbers—and 'warehouse on Chelton Street' was written there. It was clearly important."

"And?"

"I took that notepad, the entire thing, not just the top page," she said. "Then I started hunting, found a ledger in one of his drawers, a drawer that he normally kept locked, but I didn't know that. He accused me of stealing something from a locked drawer, but it wasn't locked. I didn't break into anything. But this ledger was sitting on the top of that drawer. I was too scared to really do anything much, but, since several ledgers were there, I grabbed the one on the bottom, checked through it, thought a bunch of stuff in it might be of value, and basically ran. I couldn't be at the house long. I had chosen my time frame so that he wouldn't be home. I'd waited out on the street, until he left, and I wanted to be sure to get the hell out of there before he came back. So I was pretty pressured for time when I saw this, and I grabbed it all up and ran. Only later did I review some of the items listed."

"And where is this insurance of yours?"

"That's the only thing I did right," she said. "I put it in a safe-deposit box in California."

"That's good news," he said. "But you know that more people than just you want to see that now."

"Maybe," she said. "But I needed to get out of this situation before I handed that off to anybody."

"Well, if you'd handed it off to anybody in authority," Hatch interjected, "then you might not still be in this situation because they would have picked up Max for arms dealing a long time ago."

"Maybe, but Max could have still hired kidnappers from jail," she said. "Even worse, he might never have been charged, much less jailed. If the cops came sniffing around him, Max would have figured out exactly what had been taken and by whom," she murmured. "And his *problem* would have been solved with a bullet through a window or something."

"So what do you think this kidnapping is all about?"

"I think the problem is that he wants the documents back, and he doesn't dare have me killed until he gets those from me."

"Maybe, maybe not. Maybe he thinks that, if you're killed, the matter dies anyway."

"Maybe. I don't know what my father might have said to him."

"Well, perhaps we should find that out," Killian said, and he tossed his phone to her.

She looked at it, then quickly dialed her father. She put it on speaker, as the two men remained on the other bed.

When her father answered, his voice still sounding a little tired and shaky, she said, "Dad?"

"Hey, baby," he said. "Did you have a good night?"

"I did," she said. "How about you?"

"It was okay," he said. "I'm glad that you're safe."

Stacey frowned at the phone, then at the guys.

Something odd was in her father's voice that made Killian lean forward. "Sir, are you okay?"

First came silence on the other end, and then he said, "Look after my daughter." And he hung up.

She looked over at Killian in shock. "What happened?"

"He answered that phone under duress," he said. "Your father is not alone."

CHAPTER 5

STACEY STARED AT Killian in horror, bouncing out of bed, only to cry out as the pain slammed into her. She looked over at Hatch and Killian, but both of them were already on their phones. "Please help my father," she said.

Killian nodded. "Already in progress."

"You don't understand," she said. "My father is *very* old."

"I know, and he won't handle the torture very well."

"Torture! God no," she said, aghast at the thought. She sat on the side of her bed, her hands shaking, and she thought about everything her father had been through to help her. The thought of him hurting and alone with a sadist like her husband was just too much. "Dear God," she said. "Who can I call? Who is there to help?"

"Was there anybody to help you?"

She looked at him and shook her head. "No," she said. "That's why I ran to a different country. And I drove, making sure that Max wouldn't find me by checking the airlines."

"And that's why you went to a safe-deposit box right away, correct?"

"I didn't even stay in California, just long enough to get a safe-deposit box there, then I drove on to Oregon."

"Interesting."

"I didn't want him to even know where I was," she murmured.

"Well, that was good thinking," he said, "but we'll have to backtrack your steps. We'll have to arrange to pick up your car, then the contents of your box, and we'll have to make sure that your father is okay."

"My father comes first," she said vehemently. "He's an old man, and he sure doesn't deserve this."

"I get that," Killian said gently. "We're sending men to his house right now."

She stared at him. "Like *right now*-right now or like in four hours?"

"They're nearby and already on the way." He held up his phone and said, "Remember? I have a team behind me."

"Yes, but Dad's in the States, in a completely different country."

"It doesn't matter. A phone call crosses all countries," he reminded her. "We have people we can count on to help, pretty much everywhere."

"Yes, of course." She just sat here, stunned at the turn of events.

"Would your husband have done this?"

Bitter and angry, she nodded. "It would probably be the first thing he did. And I didn't even think of that."

"And you won't worry about it now either," he said. "So he might ask your father about where something like that insurance of yours would be kept, and, if Max did, what would your father say?"

"He wouldn't know because it would be beyond him to even think about what I would do."

"Sure, but, if your father is asked, what will he say?"

"I don't know," she said quietly. "Probably a safe-deposit

box," she added, wincing.

"Well, you didn't leave it some place that Max would easily find though, right?"

"No," she said, "I chose a bank in Redding, California."

"And what banks do you normally use?"

She named two different US banks.

"So, he would check those, and he would check on your route?"

"Maybe, but he wouldn't know where I'd been," she said. "He wouldn't have any idea where I'd been."

"Unless ..." He stopped and asked, "How do you think he found you out on ... You ended up on a transport truck on a ferry, right?"

"Right."

"So ..." he said, studying her. "Any idea if you had a tracking device on you?"

She stared at him. "No, of course not. Why would I?" Just the thought of it made her sick. "He's ..." And she stopped, then said, "No, no, he wouldn't do that."

"A man who beats you up? A man who sells arms illegally? Do you really think he'll give a shit about a tracking device?"

"Well, what would it even look like?'

"It could be a tiny microdot," he said. "It would have been injected under your skin, with or without your knowledge. Although you would have had some swelling, localized at the injection site. Could have had some redness, maybe a little discomfort."

She stared at him in shock, a growing awareness inside her head. She slapped her hand to the back of her neck and said, "Check here, please."

Immediately both men bounced up and came around to

the side of the bed, where she was. Her back was turned to them, and Killian asked, "Why would you assume here?"

"It wasn't long after I was married that he told me how I got a spider bite on the back of my neck. It really bothered me for a couple days, and then it went away, and I had no reason not to believe him."

At that Killian pulled her hair gently up and away and felt under the skin. "Well, definitely something hard is there. What did you think that was?"

She used her fingertips and explored the area. "I don't really feel it even now," she said apologetically.

He rearranged her fingers to come down at another angle, and there she felt it.

"Oh my God," she cried out. "So he knows where we are right now?"

"Well, it's hard to say how much range the tracker has, but he might have tracked you to California at least."

"Jesus," she said, burying her face in her hands. It was just too much and so overwhelming. She thought she'd gotten away from him. Even though she hadn't intended on taking the material, she had. Obviously what she had taken had enraged Max, and he was willing to do almost anything to get it back. "What have I done?" she whispered to herself. "What have I done to my father?"

"Nothing," Killian said. "This is not your fault."

"Of course it is," she said bitterly. "If I hadn't taken that material, that bastard wouldn't have cared what happened, and my father would be still safe."

"We don't know for sure that your dad's not safe," he said. "Let's not panic before we know."

She stared at him. "How about we panic in a minute then, is that better?" she cried out. She bounced to her feet and immediately grabbed for the headboard. Tipping her head down, she cried out, "Get it out. Get it out!"

He looked at her and then at Hatch.

Hatch sighed and said, "I can cut it out. But I have nothing to minimize the pain."

She glared at him. "Do I look like I need anything more to minimize the pain? I already have painkillers for my leg," she said. "Get that thing out of my neck."

⚓

"WE WILL. WE will. Sit for now." Killian knew Stacey was beyond angry, and the coffee was a great relief when the knock on the door came. He opened it up and exchanged the old trolley for the new one. Sending a tip with the waiter, he closed the door again, then pushed the trolley to the table and looked at her.

"Do you want to come over here, or do you want to stay there?"

She turned her head to the side, and he saw evidence of the tears having been wiped away, but her eyes were still red. "I'll stay here," she whispered.

He poured her a cup of coffee and brought it over and said, "Here. This will help fortify you."

"Finding out my father's okay will fortify me," she said. "Nothing else."

"And I get that. But you still have to keep up your strength," he said. "We can't get you back to your father until you heal, so you need to eat."

She glared at him. "I'm not hungry."

"Your choice," he said. "We can do it the easy way or the hard way."

"What's the hard way?"

"I'll turn it into a shake, and you'll drink it."

She glared at him. "You'll shove it down my throat too?"

"You'll drink it," he said, "because you want to go see your father."

At that, he saw her resistance begin to crumble. It was a faint effort on her part, but he understood the need to fight back, to fight anything right now, when the real target of her rage and anguish wasn't in front of her.

He laced his fingers with hers and said, "Look. I'm sorry about your father. But we're on it. The men are already approaching the house, even as we speak."

Immediately her gaze flew up to his. "Do you mean that?"

"Yes," he said. "It's just a matter of what they'll find. If he's not alone, they can't take a chance of this escalating into a shooting."

"Of course not," she whispered. "Dear God."

"Stand firm," he warned. "This is not a job for the light-hearted."

"Since when is there a choice?" she said.

"There's always a choice, and, in your case," he said, "you haven't been shy of doing what you need to do. Don't give up on us now."

She snorted. "I'm not giving up."

"Agreed," he said. "So let's keep you fortified, keep you healing, and keep waiting for news."

"It's so damn hard," she cried out.

He nodded. "It is, indeed. But it's what you need to do." He returned to the trolley, lifting the lids on the trays. "We have a selection of food here," he said. "What would you like?"

"What is there?" she asked, but he was encouraged by the brighter tone in her voice.

"We have sausage, ham, and bacon in this one, with scrambled eggs here, and ... hash browns." He lifted the little dome and said, "And plenty of toast."

"Okay. I'll have some scrambled eggs, a couple sausages, a piece of bacon," she said, "and a little bit of hash browns."

He quickly served her up some food, grabbed a knife and fork, and carried it to her. Realizing that she would still struggle with eating in bed, he brought over one of the cushions from the couch and propped it under her plate, so it could rest a little bit higher. "See how that works."

"It'll be fine," she said. "I'm not in any rush to eat, so I can take my time."

"Remember that," he murmured. "It will take however long it takes. We can't speed up some things, like your healing."

"I know, but just thinking of my father dealing with that fucker is enough to make me sick."

"Got it," he murmured. "The fact is, you protected him all these years, and you can't anymore. So somewhere along the line your father has to understand just who this man Max is. And accept that the man your father thought Max was never really existed."

"It will break Dad's heart," she said. "He always prided himself on being a good judge of character."

"Chameleons exist in human form sometimes," Hatch said from the table. "He's not the first to be fooled, and he'll need to cut himself some slack over that too."

"Easier said than done," she said.

"True, and your father sounds like a man determined to be upstanding and proper and to do what's right at all times.

It's always a shock for a man like that to find out the rest of the world really doesn't give a shit about morality."

"I don't understand how they even function," she said. "To have that level of disparity between that piece-of-shit Max and what the rest of the world stands for and believes in? I just … I really don't get it. It's like Max was always living with a mask on."

"And that's exactly what he was doing," Killian said. "He wore a mask to hide who he really was. But it's more than a mask. He is a master at manipulation, at disguising his true self behind a completely different persona."

"It sucks that I didn't see through it," she said.

"Why would you?" he added. "Think about it. I mean, you're not perfect, and people don't generally go around looking for the worst in people. You couldn't have known what Max was really like. He's a pro. He made sure you had no obvious way to know that this man was somebody to avoid. You did the best you could."

"Somehow that always sounds hollow. I hear that phrase over and over again, and it sounds like a cop-out."

"I don't think it's a cop-out. I think it's a matter of taking it a little bit easier on yourself, giving yourself some grace, so that you can survive from one day to the next. Also, the way I see it, I'd rather be taken in occasionally by a con man, like Max, even if it makes me feel completely stupid. To me, it reminds me that I'm not totally cynical about the world out there, no matter how many bad examples I find. That my heart and head and values remain in the right place. That I don't automatically label everybody to be another Max. That I'll never abandon my ethics, even when the criminals seem to get away with everything." He tilted his head at her. "And I believe you know that in your heart too."

She gave him a short nod. "Maybe," she conceded.

"Stop being so hard on yourself. It doesn't help anybody."

"No, but it makes me feel better in a way," she said, with a laugh.

"Maybe, but it's also hard on everybody else."

"Are we not to expect more of ourselves then?" she asked. "Do you think I don't feel guilty, that I don't hate myself for having gotten completely suckered into Max's story, into whatever that smooth … charm of his was? It's just a con, I guess. I didn't even see it coming. Then, even when I realized it and woke up finally—after being punched in the face—I still didn't really see the depth of it."

"They ease you into it, or you'd bolt too fast." Killian shook his head, grimacing. "I'm convinced the con men out there use our sense of fair play against us, for we give them a benefit of a doubt from the get-go. When we find out we've been lied to, that loss of innocence is so painful, when our hopes and dreams crash into Max and others like him in the real world."

"It took me a little bit to understand that he meant to hurt me. Not only that he meant it but that he'd do it again, and, the longer I stayed there, the more he would beat me because he felt he could."

"Not just because he *felt* he could but he *knew* he could," Killian said. "These manipulative bullies have done this before, picking on someone smaller—like women, like children, like animals—and have never been stopped."

"Max was training you to take it, so that you would be his punching bag, and he would always have that outlet," Hatch said. "Men like that are … They know how to work it. They know what makes you afraid, and fear rules everything. Once you're terrified, he's got that much more power over you—escalating from the physical force to an emotional or psychological force—and he can do anything he wants."

"It's hard to accept though," she said quietly. "I always thought I'd be the last person to be an abused wife."

"I think every abused wife says that," Killian said quietly. "Again, don't be so hard on yourself. Guys like him, he had a lot of experience with this before you came along." He stopped, looked at her, and said, "That's a good point. Any idea if he was married before?"

She nodded. "Yes, he was."

"Name?"

"Mary is all I know," she said. "I don't know a whole lot about her or how long they were married even." She frowned at that. "Why don't I know that?"

"I don't know. Did he openly tell you about her?"

"No," she said. "He just let it slip one time."

"What? That he had an ex-wife?"

"No. Something about I'd better smarten up, that at least his first wife had finally learned. Although he said something about it took her too long, or it was too late or something like that." She frowned. "Honestly I can't remember. At the time I think I was just too damn terrified, as another blow was coming my way."

"What are the chances that he beat her too?" Killian asked.

She stared at him. "Well, considering what he did to me, I'd say the odds are very good."

"Right. So the question is, where is she now?"

With a nod from Killian, Hatch texted Jerricho that information to open an investigation into the first wife's disappearance. Not to mention organizing a raid on the

Chelton Street warehouse to see what Max was storing there. As they sat there eating, she reminisced a little bit. "It's hard to look back on the supposed good things in my marriage," she said, "because now I suspect that every trip we took was business-oriented."

"Where did you go?"

"To Switzerland three times," she said. "Cayman Islands, twice."

Killian stared at her.

She nodded. "Not too bright, was I?"

"You were woefully in love," he said. "There's a big difference."

"And I still don't know for sure what he was doing there."

"Did he have meetings?"

"Yes," she said. "I was introduced as his wife to a couple people, but it's not like I would ever recognize them again."

"You might be surprised," he said. "I wish you recognized the second kidnapper, so we could knock him off our list."

"Wouldn't that be nice," she said bitterly. "Just imagine living the way he did, always looking at somebody as an opportunity to humiliate and to plunder and to make money off of."

"Predators," Hatch said quietly from the far side. "Remember? They're always out there. They're always looking to make a buck."

"It sucks," she said.

"Absolutely. It doesn't change the fact that they exist, and they won't go away anytime soon."

Killian looked over at him. "Any luck on gathering more intel?"

"I have a lot of searches going. He's not popping up in any other countries, and facial recognition isn't giving us anything that's even close."

"Are you talking about my ex?"

Killian shook his head. "Not that we aren't searching for Max as well. No, this is the squirrelly guy I ran into earlier. We're running ID checks based on the vague description of that one man who I put a tracker on, who's no longer in the tracking area," he said. "I saw him just before the meet to get you, so I managed to slip a tracker in his pocket because he was acting suspiciously. Then he was in the exchange area after you got away. Again, pretty suspicious, but his face was mostly covered, so I couldn't give a very good description."

Just then his phone rang. He answered it in a terse tone. "That's good news, indeed," he said, his gaze flying to Stacey. He got up and walked over, holding out his phone, putting it on speaker. "Your father wants to speak with you."

"Dad?" she asked.

His voice was raspy as he whispered, "Stacey."

"Dad, are you okay?"

"I'm so sorry," he whispered. "I'm so sorry."

"What are you sorry for, Dad? What's the matter? Are you okay?"

"For not believing you," he said. "I didn't realize how evil he was."

"I know," she said. "I didn't believe it either. But he is."

"Absolutely," he said. "And I'm fine, or I will be."

"Did he hurt you?"

There was a broken laugh. "Yes, he did. And you apparently took something very important to him."

"Yes, he's dealing in arms, Dad," she said.

After a moment of silence, he said, "Wow. I never would have thought that of him. We really don't need that going on under our noses."

"Did you tell him what I had?"

"How could I? I didn't know what you had. You told me that you had proof that he was dealing with criminal activities, but you didn't tell me exactly what."

"No," she said. "I wasn't really sure myself. It's only when I stopped at a hotel overnight that I took a closer look."

"Well, I hope you have it somewhere safe," he said, "because he's after you, and he's after you in a big way."

"I'm pretty sure he was responsible for the first kidnapping," she said. "But, when I escaped on the ferry, another guy picked me up. I'm pretty damn sure he contacted Max too."

"Max did say something about enough was enough, and it was time for you to be taught a lesson and to be silenced," he said, his voice cracking. "So you need to stay safe."

"Well, as you know, I'm here with somebody who's looking after me."

"But he's coming for you, Stacey," he said. "He's coming for you. Don't you ever think he's not."

At that, she looked over at Killian, who pulled the phone closer and said, "Not to worry, sir. We're standing guard over her right now."

"That won't be enough," her father said, panic in his voice. "You don't understand what he's like. He's crazed to get that information and to silence her."

"Maybe," she said. "But I don't silence that easily, and I've had enough of his bullshit."

"Right," her father said. "You had the courage to flee from the abuse, which I didn't even understand. But I think he was just playing with you back then, compared to what he'll do when he catches you now."

CHAPTER 6

STACEY FELT THE chills running down her shoulders and arms, long after ending the phone call. She looked at the two men. "I have to get home."

"Yeah, and why is that?" Killian asked, looking at her. He had been doing as much research on her husband as he could.

"My father's still not out of danger."

"Your father now has the Secret Service protecting him," he said. "Which is a lot better than what he had before. Your husband doesn't care about your father, beyond hurting or killing him to hurt you. I'm surprised Max didn't take your father on a road trip to help flush you out."

"That's what I was wondering myself," she said. "The bottom line is, you can't trust what Max'll do from any one day to the next."

"Predators are like that," Hatch repeated.

She glared at him. "That's not helpful."

"No," he said, and he flipped his laptop around. "Is this his buddy?"

She looked at it and nodded. "Yeah, that's James Dean."

"Also known as Mark Leif, aka Lyon Hamilton."

She stared at him.

"Interpol is very interested in his location. He's from South America—Colombia, to be exact. And apparently he's been a very bad boy."

"But he's living in Texas, near my husband, right down the block," she protested.

"And that tells you something about the relationship between them."

"I still don't get it," she said.

"Chances are, the weapons are going to Colombia."

"But that's not fair," she said. "If they should be going anywhere, it should be to help the poor people get away from guys like him."

"It doesn't matter where they're going. It's illegal, and, chances are, he's selling to the highest bidder—or playing one against another. And another government will either get wiped out or the poor people will get stomped into the ground," he said. "It never seems that we fund the right side."

"I … I don't know," she said. "I've never seen anything to make me think that James Dean had any Colombian connections."

"Does he travel a lot?"

"Yes," she said. "I think so. He's into import-export stuff, if …" The words slowly slipped out of her mouth, as she sagged back. "Oh, that makes so much more sense," she said. "He was always telling me how he was going to South America. I just wasn't thinking Colombia was his destination."

"Yeah, definitely South America. So, now that we have somebody wanted on Interpol's watch list," he said, "this will ramp up in a big way."

"Can you get more men then?"

Killian looked at her in astonishment. "Why would I want more men?"

She stared at him in shock. "Well, to help catch these two."

"That's not the way we typically work. See? The problem with more men is, then we have to coordinate with more men, and more men can mess up," he said. "Much better we keep our operation small."

"That's two men to catch two men, if you're trying to just get Max and James," she said. "Max has the money to hire a dozen men. If it's just you two against twelve plus Max and James, the odds are really good that none of us will survive."

Killian shook his head, and the smile at the corner of his mouth made her heart ache. Ache for better things. Ache for a new life, a new relationship, and a time of peace and quiet, where she didn't have to look over her shoulder or to be afraid, … afraid of that fist coming at her again. Though now a punch in the face was the least of her problems.

She gave herself a mental shake and turned her gaze to Hatch to see the same look on his face. "You're both acting like I'm insulting you," she said, facing Killian again.

"Well, you are actually," Killian murmured. "But that's okay."

"Maybe it's not okay," she said. "But this is, … this is all just too unbelievable."

"I hear you, but the fact of the matter is, we would much rather keep our main unit small and simple. That way we can control everything, and we don't have as many ways to potentially screw up then. We have backup teams helping us already."

She sagged back into the bed. "Well, I can help too," she said. "Or I can once I'm back on my feet again."

"No," he said. "Not happening. You'll rest, and we'll run

this op ourselves."

"Dammit," she said. "It's hardly an operation. We're just holed up in a hotel room."

Killian grinned at her. "Don't you worry," he said. "We got this covered."

"Okay," she warned, "but I think you're taking on too much, and, if I feel the need, I'll call the police."

"No," he said in a firm voice. "You're not. We have to trust that you trust us. Have we steered you wrong yet?"

She thought about the men who had found her, not only in a vehicle parked in the middle of the Canadian woods but found her in the brush afterward and then had saved her, yet again. "No," she said quietly. "I trust you."

"All the way, no matter what?" Killian asked.

Something more was in his tone of voice. Something they needed to hear. She nodded. "You haven't steered me wrong yet," she said.

"And we won't," he said. "We came to rescue you. That's our job. But now that we realize the bigger picture is a further threat, it won't be enough to just rescue you. We have to get your ex. We need to pick up James Dean, and we also need to find the second kidnapper."

"What about the pair of men in my first kidnapping?"

"I wouldn't be surprised if Max hasn't already killed them," Killian said. When she gasped, he added, "Sorry. I'm used to working with my team, and we tend to be blunt."

At that, Hatch spoke up. "Any chance that this second kidnapper was already connected to Max or James?" he asked her.

"Well, the second kidnapper obviously contacted my ex—given my IDs in my purse. Oh, shit. Max is my contact person still, damn it. Forgot about that. Because the second kidnapper said that he was supposed to kill me, per Max, and that my ex would be pissed off if he didn't do the job because he'd already accepted the money. He was trying to play it both ways and get paid by you too. He was scared enough of my ex not to let me go with you, but I don't know if he was scared enough of Max to come back and take care of business or not."

"You might be surprised," he said. "Max could always sweeten the pot, by upping the money."

"And that would probably work too because this guy was obviously motivated by money. I just don't know why. And he's bound to be really pissed that he didn't get your ransom money."

"A lot of people are motivated by money," Hatch said. "What is there to question about it?"

"I don't know," she said. "I just didn't think so many predators were out there, feeding on the innocent."

"Well, we've already established that there are," Killian said. "What we need to do is find a way to shake them out of the woodwork, so we can put this to rest, once and for all."

"Is that even possible now, when, instead of my ex, it's my ex plus others?" she asked.

"Your ex, plus his friend James Dean, plus whoever the second asshole is, yes," Killian said, and then he rubbed his hands together and gave her a big grin. "We do love a challenge."

She rolled her eyes. "You might like a challenge," she said, "but I don't want to be the spoils that go to the winner or to find out that I chose the wrong side in this war."

"There are no sides," he said. "There are just the winners. And that's us."

She laughed. "If nothing else," she said, "you two are

confident."

"That comes from years of experience," Killian said quietly. "Don't worry. We'll look after you."

And she had to be satisfied with that.

He looked over at Hatch. "We need answers, and we need answers now."

Just then came a knock on the door.

⚓

IMMEDIATELY KILLIAN STOOD, motioned to Stacey, and whispered, "Be quiet."

She just raised an eyebrow.

He raced to the door and stood behind it, as Hatch got up and walked over.

Hatch pulled the door open and said, "Hey."

"A parcel was delivered to the reception area," said the man at the door.

"Oh, really? We're not expecting anything," Hatch said, keeping his hands down.

"Well, it came delivered by courier, for you."

"A local courier?"

"Yeah, it's not my deal. Here, you have it," he said, and he shoved it into Hatch's arms. There was exasperation in the other man's voice.

Hatch took it, as the other man strode off, muttering, "Some people."

"Hey," Hatch called to the hotel clerk, "did you get an ID on the courier who delivered it?"

"I said it was the local courier." Then he disappeared down the stairwell.

Hatch closed the door and turned toward Killian. "I

don't like the sound of that."

"Me either. It also means that, like Stacey said, we're compromised."

She jerked upright. "We didn't get the tracker out yet either."

"Nope," he said. "So we'll do that right now." Killian walked over, and she turned her back to him, still in bed. He pulled back her hair, and he said, "Hold your hair up here."

"Okay, but it'll hurt, won't it?"

He pinched the skin just above where the tracker was. "Does that hurt?"

"That's not too bad."

He made a sharp clean slice. She yelped. He said, "It's already done."

"No," she gasped, struggling to control her breathing. "It's not done. You haven't got it out yet."

He pinched the space just below it and out slid the tracker. Holding it on the end of his thumbnail, he showed it to her, right under her nose.

"That's it?" she asked, incredulous.

"That's it," he said. "Let me clean this up and put a bandage on your neck." He walked to the table and dropped the tracker in front of Hatch, who was running a series of tests on the box just delivered to them. "Let me know if you find anything on this bug too," Killian told Hatch.

"You'll be the second one," he said. "There're are no explosives so that's good."

With that, Killian detoured into the bathroom, grabbed the disinfectant from the hotel's standard medical kit, and, after swabbing her neck, he showed her a Mickey Mouse bandage. He chuckled. "Just what you want, kid bandages." And he gently placed it over her newest wound.

"I don't really care," she said, "but we need to move and now."

"It's already been ordered," Killian said. "I'm just waiting on a location."

She looked at him and said, "I can't run. You know that."

"I know," he said calmly. Then he added, "Go ahead and pack up your stuff."

She looked at him, nodded, and slowly stood up. "That tracker has been in my neck for eighteen months," she said.

"Yep," he said. "But, the great news is, it's out. So wherever we go from here, Max won't have a clue. And I don't think this has the range he was hoping for."

"But it did. Max found us here. He delivered us that damn package," Stacey said, pointing, her voice rising.

"Not Max necessarily," Killian said. "Could be the second kidnapper or that guy in town I lost my tracker on."

"See?" Stacey said. "That doesn't mean that somebody else coming into town doesn't have a tracker."

"Would Max have traced your phone?"

"Probably." She snorted. "With a tracker in my neck, hell yes, Max would have tracked my phone."

"Regardless," Killian said, "we'll get you a new one."

"And now that we have this tracker out of my neck, as soon as we move, we should be good, right?"

"Yes," he said. He looked over at Hatch. "What's in the box?"

Hatch had the delivery open now. He held up an electronic device. "It's a recording." He hit Play, and a video showed up. Hatch's face turned grim. "It's your father," he said. "You don't want to see this."

"Do you think Max took it before my father was rescued, or is Dad in danger yet again?"

Hatch shook his head. "Don't know. This was sent this morning."

"But Dad's safe now, right?" She looked from Killian to Hatch. "I need to talk to him." She turned and looked at Killian. "I need to talk to my father again." Immediately he held out his phone to her and said, "Just redial the last call on this phone."

"Right." She took a deep breath and then quickly phoned her father.

"I'm fine," he reassured her. "Now you get out of there."

"We're going."

She handed the phone back to Killian and said, "You need to deep-six that."

"Oh, I will," he said. "Come on. Let's go."

While she'd been talking to her father, Killian and Hatch had packed up the room. She quickly made her way to the door as fast as she could. Killian stepped out first. When she joined him in the hallway, she was relieved to see that it was empty, but she couldn't get her anger and that feeling that this would all go badly out of her mind.

"Come on," he said. And he led her to an elevator at the far end.

"Why couldn't we have taken a closer one?" she asked, moving slowly.

"Because this is a service elevator, and it goes straight down to the parking level."

"But we didn't park down there."

"No," he said. "But that's where our new vehicle is."

She followed them, and the trio quickly made their way downstairs, where she was placed comfortably into a small van. Once she was seated, the two men stowed their bags, hopped into the front seat, and they pulled out.

"Jesus," she said. "I still feel like we're being tracked, like we're being followed, and we'll meet a boogeyman around every corner."

"Listen. You're reacting to the latest news, finding out that you've had a tracking device in your neck this whole time. That is incredibly intrusive when done without your knowledge. Now your father's been introduced to the real Max. Here's the thing. You won't feel safe until you are. Until your dad is. Until we end this once and for all."

"I can't wait," she whispered. "I just can't wait."

⚓

WITH ALL THREE in the new vehicle, the two guys keeping track of their surroundings, Killian quickly drove toward the exit in the underground parking lot. As he did, two other vehicles screeched to intersect his path. He swore, shifting into Reverse, and headed backward, swinging around again, looking for another exit. One vehicle seemed to follow him, but the other remained just inside the lot.

"What if there's only one exit?" she cried out from the back seat.

"That's fine," Killian said. "I just need more room to ramp up, before I hit them."

She gasped and said, "Are you talking about ramming them?"

"If they don't move, yes."

As it was, he made several quick sharp maneuvers and came out ahead of one, with another still blocking the exit. "Hold on, Stacey." Killian quickly jumped the curb, leaving through the Do Not Enter lane and raced away from both.

"Who are they?" she asked, as she twisted in the back seat to look.

He studied the view behind him from the rearview mirror and said, "I'm not sure. I wish we had cameras that would give us an insight into what just happened."

Beside him, Hatch said, "I'm on it."

Killian drove hard and fast, taking a lot of corners and back alleys in order to avoid whatever pursuit might be happening behind him.

"How far away are we from our next spot?" she asked worriedly.

"Fifteen minutes."

"In fifteen minutes, you can probably get across this whole town," she said. "Are you sure it's safe, where we're going, I mean?"

"It's safe," he said. "At the moment. Of course, if we get found out, then it'll be the next unsafe place." At that, she went quiet. He felt sorry for her because there wouldn't be any easy answers for this. It was getting more and more difficult, as people came out of the woodwork after them. He had to wonder if it wasn't the husband. "We need to contact Max," Killian said suddenly.

"Why?" she asked. "Anything my ex says is nothing you can believe."

"That might be true, but we still have to see if it's him behind this."

"You mean, he might make a deal for me?"

"That's what I'm wondering."

A long moment passed before she said hesitantly, "You ... You wouldn't really turn me over, would you?"

"Of course not," he said. "But we have to know, we have to find out exactly who and what we're dealing with."

"Says you," she said. "I'm okay to not see whoever it is."

"I understand. However, you don't want to spend the rest of your life watching your back, do you?"

"I'm afraid that horse is already out of the barn," she said flippantly. "Does anybody ever get over something like this?"

"If you get closure, yes," he said, as he took another sharp turn. He took two more sharp turns, before heading out to a long stretch of road, where he immediately shut off his lights, yet continued driving.

In the complete darkness, she gasped and asked, "Is that safe?"

"It's safer than giving anybody a trail to follow," he said, speaking quietly in the hum of the darkness. Killian knew that he'd lost whoever was behind them, but that didn't mean they wouldn't come up against them again. He drove another ten minutes, heading out of town to one of the other communities. As he approached one of the main lights, he turned on his headlights again and took a left. Then he took a right, followed by two more lefts.

"So we're right back where we started from," she said good-naturedly.

"Not quite."

"But obviously we're somewhere."

Just like that, he took several more corners, then suddenly pulled into a back alley and then into an open garage. The door closed swiftly behind them. Hatch left the vehicle immediately. Killian let out a slow breath, then turned and looked at her. "Are you okay?"

"I am," she said. "I guess we can't get a fast airport flight out of here, huh?"

"No, not with that leg. Let's get you inside, where you can get rested again. That's what you need in order to get out of here."

"I'm starting to feel like I'm putting you guys in danger now."

"Not your concern," he said. He moved quickly to help her get out of the back. Keeping her leg still without jarring it or bumping the bandaged area, he pulled her against him, then slowly lowered her, to the floor. "You're still in your shorts and a T-shirt."

She shrugged. "I didn't have time to change of out my PJs."

"Hey, as long as you're comfortable with it, I'm good." He grabbed the rest of the bags from the back seat and led the way toward the inner access door.

Hatch stood there, waiting for them. "Inside is clear. I'll do a search of the exterior of the house."

"Good, and we'll set the security afterward." Killian led Stacey inside to the kitchen, then through to a small sitting area. "Two bedrooms on the main floor," he said. "So we'll stay down here."

"Okay," she said, but her voice was fainter than he'd have liked.

He looked at her sharply, seeing her pale skin, her huge eyes. "Are you all right?"

"Yeah," she murmured. "It's just that everything, well, it feels *off*."

"Yeah, I'm sure it does. And that's okay."

She collapsed on the couch with her leg resting on the big ottoman, and he walked into the little kitchen and said, "How about a cup of tea?"

"That'd be lovely," she said. "I feel like I'll crash again soon too."

"That's the adrenaline rush, draining from you," he said.

"You're safe now."

"For how long though?" she said, soft and low. "Also what about everybody else in my life?"

"Is there anybody else you're close to, other than your father?"

She stopped, thought about it, and then gave a hard snort. "Not so much, now that you mention it," she said. "My husband didn't approve of any of my friends. And, when I left him, I didn't want to contact anybody because they had warned me to stay away from him. I hadn't listened, and I just couldn't face all the *I told you so*s I knew I had coming."

"Well, if they were true friends," Killian said, "they might have said *I told you so* once, but then they should have left it alone. And honestly? Real friends would have come looking for you and would have opened their arms to help you. So maybe you're better off without them after all."

"I don't even know who I am anymore," she said. "It's been such an incredible change in my world. And maybe that's not such a bad thing either," she said quietly.

"Maybe not."

She looked down at her leg. "This damn leg is causing a lot of trouble."

"Which is exactly why the kidnapper did it," he said. "Because you're incapacitated, so you can't escape. You can't do much of anything, except struggle with the injury."

"So is this something he's done before, you think?"

He looked at her in surprise and then slowly nodded his head.

"Now that's a line of work a guy can be really proud of," she said in disgust, thinking of other women with big gashes in their legs. "It's not like you can track that."

"*Hmm,*" he said, pulling out his phone and looking down, as he sent off messages to his team. "You might be surprised just what they can track." With that done, he walked back into the kitchen and then called out, "I said tea, but would you rather have coffee instead?"

"Either is fine," she said. "Just a hot comforting drink sounds great."

He put on the kettle and then made a pot of coffee as well.

By the time that was done, Hatch had returned to the kitchen and gave him a nod. "All clear. Security set."

"Perfect."

"How long can we stay here?" she asked them.

"Several days hopefully," they said.

"You mean, long enough for me to heal?"

"Long enough that you can tolerate the trip down south."

"If it wasn't a commercial airline," she said, "it would be easier."

"It won't be a civilian airline for sure, and it will be easier for us to restrict who is around you," he said. "But you still have to be ready for it. That car ride couldn't have been comfortable, even in a roomy SUV. Imagine flying for hours at a time, and all that getting in and out of the planes. It'll hurt your leg, for sure. So let's give it a couple more days, and I promise we'll try to get you on a military flight and get you back to California first. We'll figure out how to get your car back to you somehow."

"I would love that," she said, as she shifted on the couch among a bunch of pillows, propping up her head on them. "Why am I always so dang tired?"

"Because of the pills, the injuries, the shock, and the

adrenaline. It all just crashes you," he said in a laughing tone. "Just remember. The best healing happens when you are asleep, so think of it as a good thing and leave it at that."

"Okay," she said. "I'll do some healing, and I'll be wanting coffee when I wake up."

He chuckled. "Go ahead. Close your eyes and get some rest." He watched as she closed her eyes and immediately fell into a deep sleep, long before her tea or coffee. He turned to look at Hatch and said, "We need to track down other women who were cut like Stacey was. It's a hell of a tactic in terms of keeping a prisoner in check and making her incapable of running away. I just wonder how many times he might have done that before."

"We need to find that out," Hatch said, turning to look at her. "And in what states, what countries?"

"I know. We'll start with the US West Coast right now, and I suspect that's probably his hunting ground."

"So we need to expand that to check from the Yukon all the way down the west coast of Canada into the US."

"I've put the team on it," Killian said, "but it wouldn't hurt if we dug into it ourselves. I'll take California," he said, turning to look at her. "Maybe you should start in British Columbia, as the guy picked her up off a ferry there."

"On it," Hatch replied.

Killian's phone buzzed. "It's Jerricho," he noted to Hatch. "What's up?"

"We're monitoring the police chatter in your area and seems someone was caught speeding. He tried to tell the cops that a man's wife had been kidnapped by two men, and he and his buddy were sent to your hotel to save her."

"Not very original but it delayed us for a bit."

"Stay low until you are ready for transport. Meanwhile,

we put in an anonymous tip that these were hired guns and gave them Max and James as possible leads. We'll share more with the locals as you and the team uncover more. I understand the guy already in custody is giving up his partner involved in this. The police expect to have him in custody soon."

"Sounds good. Keep us updated."

They both poured coffees and headed to the dining room table, where they set up their laptops and got to work. It wasn't too much longer that Killian looked over at Hatch. "Last year, a woman filed a kidnapping complaint, and her kidnapper attacked her by cutting up her leg so badly that she couldn't get away. He didn't sexually assault her, eventually dropped her off on the roadside. She said that he was looking for ransom, but she didn't have anybody who would pay. He had thought she was somebody else, so it was a case of mistaken identity. She said that she's still haunted by his actions and by the injury that has kept her close to home, even after all this time."

"Well, that definitely sounds like one right there. When and where was that?"

They jotted down her info on a sheet of paper and kept looking, and it wasn't long before they had five cases.

"Five cases, five women, all kidnapped, all with the same cuts to the leg," Hatch noted, shaking his head. "Wow."

"The good news is," Killian said, "that they were all released without further harm."

"So at least he didn't kill them." Hatch nodded.

"Now, in Stacey's case," Killian said, "she did say that her second kidnapper was supposed to kill her because that's what Max paid him for. But the kidnapper didn't do that. He got greedy, trying to score our cash as well. So he doesn't seem to be a murderer either, from what we know to date. And these five cases could be his as well. But surely Max is looking for that second kidnapper who took Max's money and didn't get the job done, but, more than that, Max is looking for Stacey."

"Max may take care of our second kidnapper problem."

Killian agreed. "And then there's the first two kidnappers themselves, trying to get out of trouble with Max for losing Stacey, maybe trying to clean up any loose threads there."

"I wonder if her father is a loose end?"

"I wonder …" At that, Killian quickly punched an order into the Mavericks' text box, to make doubly sure that her father was adequately guarded, and the response came back immediately that he was and would be until the case was over with. He looked up and said, "They've got it covered."

"Okay, that should have been a given."

"Nothing is a given in this world," Killian said, "so I always double-check just to make sure we do the best we can and make no assumptions without verification where we can get it."

CHAPTER 7

STACEY WOKE UP the next morning, her body stiff and achy from head to toe. She remembered falling asleep on the couch, yet she was in a bed now. *Killian must have moved me.* She laid still for a long moment, as she tried to assess if anything else had happened. But she figured it was just from the rough ride away from the hotel and from the added psychological stress of moving from one location to another. She slowly sat up, pushing aside the bedcovers and swinging her injured leg outward to drop to the floor, gauging her strength levels. She made her way to the bathroom, wincing as she realized the bandage was covered in blood again. She hadn't gotten it changed last night, and now she needed a shower, and it would obviously have to come off.

She studied it for a long moment. What the heck. She might as well have a shower and take it off there. After all, getting it wet first made taking off the bandage less painful. Then Killian could rebandage it fresh, after she got dressed. It was morning outside, and she heard the birds, and the sun shone brightly. She turned on the shower, and, as soon as it was hot and ready, she stepped in, with the bloody bandage still affixed. She scrubbed her body down, avoiding the bandage on most of her thigh, taking the time to lather her hair twice, letting the water sluice down her face and onto her back. She already felt better as she got clean again.

With the soap and warm water easing off the dried blood, she gingerly took off the bandage, wincing as she could still see dry crusty blood everywhere. On the whole, the incision looked decent though. She let the water soak down into the wound and around, cleaning it up. The hot water felt good, easing the tension in her leg. As soon as she was done, she grabbed one of the towels and dried off as much as she could, patting around the wound. Then she wrapped one towel around her hair, while she grabbed another for her body.

As soon as she made her way back to her bedroom, she laid out what she had for clothing and managed to get partially dressed in a T-shirt and panties. She chose shorts again, as she didn't have any other clothes that allowed for the bandaging to be done. Slowly she managed to slip the shorts up over her injured leg. Now fully dressed and in need of a fresh bandage, she straightened up her room, then headed to find the guys. She was still braiding her hair as she walked into the kitchen.

Both men sat there, and they looked up in surprise.

"What?" she said. "Were you expecting me to sleep later?"

"That, and the fact that you're walking so easily," Killian said.

She nodded. "The hot shower helped a lot."

He got up and took a closer look at the leg. "It looks pretty decent, but I'd still like to see another bandage on it, to help from hurting you and to avoid infection. You'll need to keep up the antibiotics for the same reason."

"I won't argue with that," she said. "I took off the old one in the shower. It was pretty crusty with dried blood. I gave it all a good cleaning, but I think another bandage would be good for today."

"Give me a minute," he said, and he disappeared.

She looked over at Hatch. "How was your morning?"

"It's good," he said. "Just checking up on the news."

"Anything about the kidnappers?"

"Nope."

She looked around at the table and saw all kinds of notes and files. "Did you guys learn anything new?"

"Maybe," he said. "Do you want a coffee?" he asked.

She nodded. "Yes, please, I'd appreciate it." She sat down on the bench, waiting for Killian to come back. "What did you find out?" she asked.

"A bunch of stuff, not anything terribly awe-inspiring," Hatch said. "The two guys working the parking lot are in custody, so you don't have to worry about them." She nodded, her mouth grim. "Just a couple locals, probably hired by Max. We're leaving that to the police to investigate. However, it looks like the guy who kidnapped you from the ferry has potentially done this before."

"Well, it makes sense," she said. "He had no hesitation about grabbing me instead of helping me. Who does that?"

"We have five related cases so far," he said.

Her jaw dropped. "Five?"

"Five women were kidnapped, their legs slashed open while he had them, but they were all released when ransom money was paid."

"So, this is how he makes his living?" she said in disbelief. "And he cuts all the women he kidnaps?"

"It would appear to be his standard operating procedure," he said.

It was stunning to think that somebody could have gotten away with this so many times. "And the women could never identify him?"

"No, they couldn't," he said. "In each case it happened the same way. They were snatched from an innocuous setting, and then the family was contacted for ransom."

"Which is when my father was contacted. But, instead of paying online, he sent you guys in person," she said.

"Yeah, and rightly so. Paying ransom rarely works out for anybody but the kidnapper. The good news about this guy is that he didn't kill any of his victims."

"That is really good news," she said. And then she stopped, winced, and added, "At least as far as you know."

He looked at her with a flat stare and said, "Yes, as far as we know, with the cases we've found to date."

"I really don't want to think of this guy having done this to any other victims. How does the timeline look for them?"

"Well, that's why it's a bit of an issue," he said. "We found five so far. But that's just between Oregon and Washington State."

"So what about Canada?" she asked. "That's where I was taken from, both times. There could be another five women from BC or from the territories or even Alaska." She then challenged, "How about California?"

"Exactly, the results are ongoing."

"Do you know how much the ransom was that he asked of my father?"

"That's one of the unique things about it that keeps him kind of under the radar and prompts people to pay. He doesn't ask for all that much."

"Like how much?"

"In these five cases we've found, apparently around the five grand mark."

"So something that families might raise as a ransom, and yet not so far out of line that it's out of the question."

"Exactly," he said.

"And fifty grand for a weekend's work?" she said bitterly. "That's a pretty damn decent wage."

"It certainly is," Hatch said, with a nod.

Just then Killian returned with a metal first aid kit. "Did you get coffee?"

She lifted her cup and smiled. "Hatch got me a cup."

"Good," he said. "Let's get that leg bandaged." He quickly redressed it, and, when he was done, she swung her leg back under the table, and he sat back down in front of his laptop and the other paperwork.

"Hatch was just telling me about the five other cases."

"Yes," he said. "Although we're looking for more."

"Did you check the morgue?" she asked in a hard voice.

"Meaning, cases where he may have killed the women?"

"Well, I mean, it seems a little bit hard to believe that he would have had success with every case. Some women will fight and not stop fighting."

"And that's quite true," he said. "But it should still be in the case files."

"Not if they're unsolved, would it?"

"Well, it's one of the searches that we've asked for, but we haven't got any answers back yet," he said.

"Right, we always expect information to be right at our fingertips these days, don't we?"

"We certainly do," he said. "But it's not all that easy to get sometimes."

"No, you're quite right there," she murmured. She sat here with her coffee and asked, "Are we cooking our own food here or …"

"The kitchen's fully stocked, and you should stay off that leg as much as you can," Killian said. "So I can cook you whatever you would you like."

"Steak and eggs," she said immediately.

Surprised, he answered, "Okay, so maybe not steak."

"Well, then how about something like ham and eggs, bacon and eggs, some toast? I'm really hungry," she said.

"Well, being hungry is a really good sign," he said, with a bright smile. "So let me just close up some of this, and I'll get you something started."

"Well, not just me though," she said. "Aren't you guys eating?"

"We'll all eat," he said firmly. "We're all in this together."

"Well, I'm glad you think so," she said, with a crooked smile. "And, you guys, I'm really grateful not to be alone. I don't think anything is worse than waking up as a captive, knowing that nobody cares, that nobody wants to help you, that nobody can help you because they don't even know the situation you're in. It just makes you feel so alone."

"I can imagine," he said gently. "And I'm sorry that happened to you. Obviously that's a horrible scenario."

"It is, and it just, it's just a feeling that I still haven't quite shed."

"Well, you're not alone now," he said. "So keep that thought in mind."

"I know," she said gently. "And again, I really appreciate it."

"Maybe you should be thanking your father for that too," he said, "because he's the one who contacted us."

"Oh, I will," she said, "and hopefully this will heal the rift between us."

"And was this rift big enough that it couldn't heal before?"

"No, I don't think so," she said. "It was so frustrating because, once I realized what I was up against in my marriage, I guess I was looking for his support, and he just couldn't give it to me. It was beyond his comprehension that my husband could be like that. My father is a righteous man and, as such, loves his daughter, so expects his son-in-law to love me too. This won't be an easy thing for my dad to come to terms with. Because he'll also have to come to terms with the fact that, by not listening, he may have had a hand in me getting hurt. Yet I wouldn't want him to think like that. It's totally not his fault."

"No, but you know how it is when it comes to guilt sometimes. We're really good at making sure we fit the mold, so that we can take on as much of it as we need to."

"But that doesn't do anybody any good," she said. "He's not responsible for this."

"Well, neither are you. Remember that. Your husband ultimately started this nightmare," he said. "So you can expect that your father is likely to feel as if he could have prevented it, at least."

She sighed and sat back. "I guess, but that's not how I want him to feel."

"Maybe not," he said. "So, when you get a chance, you can tell him that you don't hold him responsible for this and see if you can let him off the hook. Chances are, he won't be quite so easy to let himself off."

She nodded. "I think you're right," she said. "But, I mean, all's well that ends well, right?"

"Maybe, but first, let's get you home, safe and sound."

She smiled at that. "So, about that bacon and eggs?"

He rolled his eyes. "Nothing like having a hungry female to feed," he joked.

"Hey, I'm just asking for food," she said. "It could have been an entirely different kind of hunger."

He looked at her, one eyebrow raised, and said, "Now that kind of hunger, I'd be totally down for."

She snorted. "Oh, right, well, that's not happening. Besides, I'm injured."

He laughed. "Well, that will be an excuse for a day or two but not after that."

"Isn't that against some rescuer code? Besides, you'll soon be off into the wild blue yonder anyway," she said. "Living the life that you always live."

"Which would mean another mission," he said, with a laugh.

She looked at him in surprise. "Don't you ever get downtime?"

"Yep," he said. "Sometimes. Why?"

She shook her head. "I was just thinking it might be nice to take you guys out for a beer afterward, or something, as a thank-you gesture."

"You're right. It would be nice, but it's certainly not necessary. We don't even live in the same states."

She looked back and forth from one to the other. "Really?"

They shook their heads. "Nope, I'm from California. Hatch's from Wisconsin."

"So you just meet up on jobs then?" she asked. "Okay, I'm not sure how to deal with that information."

"Does that bother you?"

"Well, it shouldn't," she said, "but, for some reason, it kind of does, yes."

He laughed. "Well, don't let it."

"It's odd, but I thought you guys were probably great friends—in real life, I mean."

At that, both men looked at her in surprise.

She shrugged. "I know. That doesn't sound right either."

"This *is* real life," Killian said gently.

"I know that," she said briskly. "I don't know what I'm trying to say."

"Outside of missions, we are friends," Killian said. "We used to work together in the navy."

"Used to? I thought you were still there."

"We're in the special operations division now."

She said, with a smile, "Well, that makes a little more sense." As she watched, Killian got up, packed up his stuff, and closed his laptop. "Oh, goody. Food finally," she said.

He burst out laughing. "Are you really that hungry?"

She shrugged, as she drained her coffee. "Another couple cups of this and I'll probably not eat anything."

"Well, we can't have that," he said. "Your body needs sustenance."

"Does it though? It feels like it needs to rest," she said. "My mind too, with everything just spinning around in my head. I mean, I figured it was my husband originally, but then that second attack? That one really gets me. It was, like, so demoralizing. It's bad enough that I was out there suffering and struggling to survive. But to think that, of all the people who could have seen me on that ferry and who could have come to my rescue, who do I get? Another predator. And that's a bit beyond me, and frankly, I'm struggling with it. Now I feel like the ratio of good guys to bad guys is different than I thought, and now I'll have to look at everybody differently out there, wondering if they're safe, wondering who'll attack me next."

"That's a perfectly normal reaction after what you've gone through," Hatch said in a serious tone. "It's hard not to think about what's happening out there and who's out to get you. All I can tell you is that the feeling does fade, but, in a way, it's good if it doesn't completely because you still really should be aware. You want to enjoy the world out there but still keep an eye out," he said. "Finding that healthy balance, well, that'll take some time."

"I would just like to hit a Delete button or something and wipe out the last three days."

"Well, how about the last two years, with your husband?"

"That would be nice too," she said, with a heavy sigh. "When you get married, you go into it with such high hopes, an almost giddy sense of expectation. Then, when you come back down to reality, it took me such a long time, and then I had this slow dawning realization that he really was a monster, hiding within such a pretty disguise. I just—I just didn't see it. Until it was far too late. And, because I didn't see it, I can't trust my own judgment."

"That will change too," Killian said. "When you make new decisions, new judgments, they'll be more positive and easier to handle."

"I'm not so sure," she said softly.

"Well, let me know if you need more coffee," he said. "I'm working on the bacon."

She lifted her nose as the bacon hit the pan, and she heard the sizzle, almost like a crossover of senses. "What is it about bacon?" she marveled.

"I'm not sure," Killian said, "but it's almost universal."

She nodded. "And I, for one, am very grateful for that."

"Well, we'll get you fed here in a few minutes."

"What's the plan for today?" she asked, changing the subject abruptly.

"Stay here and rest," he said. "Did you have anything else you wanted to do?"

"No," she said. "I'll sleep and rest, then rest and sleep."

"That sounds like the same thing, but both are very doable."

And that's how the day went. She napped; she got up, walked around a few minutes until her leg started killing her. She laid down, watched some TV, got up, went to bed, crashing for a nap when needed. Then it was just a repeat, rinse, and repeat. By the time dinner rolled around, she looked at the guys and said, "I'm not even hungry. It seems like all we've done today is sit around on our butts and eat."

"Well, you," he said, with a big grin, "have slept a lot too."

"I have, and I'm grateful for that," she said. "It must be the pills."

"I would imagine so," he said. "They do tend to make people sleepy."

"When your body needs to heal, I suppose that's probably not a bad thing," she said.

"Exactly."

Yet, when dinner was ready, she sat there and ate until she was full and then groaned. "I can't believe I'm tired again," she said, yawning. "Or that I ate all that."

He just nodded and said, "Don't forget to take your pills before you go to bed."

"Well, maybe if I don't take my pills," she said, "I could make it through tomorrow, more awake than asleep."

"And maybe making it through tomorrow isn't the

goal," he said.

She shrugged, took her pills, and headed to bed. With any luck, she would have a little bit more energy tomorrow. Her last thought as she crashed was that, at least this way, she was getting stronger faster. So maybe the next time she came up against one of these assholes, she would get away on her own.

The next morning, the phone rang and woke her up. The smell of bacon hit her nose, making her stomach growl. She made her way out to the sitting area and sat down on the couch. She watched Hatch, as he answered Killian's phone. She looked back at Killian. "Do you want to take that, and I can watch the bacon?"

He shrugged and said, "Hatch is fine with my phone."

She half listened to Hatch's conversation but didn't get most of it. Irritated and annoyed for some reason, she hopped up, walked over slowly to where the chef was cooking, and stole a piece of bacon off a plate, where it was cooling.

He lightly smacked her fingers.

"I'm really hungry," she murmured.

"It'll be ready in a few minutes," he said.

"So, what are we doing today?" she asked.

"More of the same," was his reply.

She groaned. "I don't think I can do more of that. It was pretty boring yesterday."

"How would you know?" he said, with a chuckle. "You slept all day."

She thought about it and agreed. "Can I call my dad again?"

"Yep, you sure can. As soon as Hatch is off my phone."

She saw an odd look on Hatch's face. "Uh-oh," she said,

as Killian looked at her, and she pointed in Hatch's direction.

Killian twisted to look at Hatch, immediately shut off the bacon, moved the pan off the burner, and snatched the phone. "Repeat that."

She listened again, hearing only part of it.

"That's fine," he said. "We'll handle it."

He turned, looked at her, and said, "Your father was taken."

"Jesus," she said, staring at him. "What does that mean?"

"Meaning," he said, "he was kidnapped."

"It must have been my ex," she said. "I thought you said Dad was safe, protected." She couldn't get the shock or anger out of her voice.

"We assumed so."

"Well, how was it possible?" she cried out. "That bastard Max will kill him."

"No," Killian said. "That he will not do. But he is quite likely to use him as bait, to get you back into his control."

She stared at him, not comprehending.

"A trade," he said. "He'll want to trade you for your father."

"Let's do it," she said, instantly straightening and pushing away from the stove.

"No," he said. "No can do."

"You have to," she roared. "You can't let my father die over this."

"I wasn't planning on it," he said. "But what we can't do is hand you over to get hurt, or worse, killed."

She slumped down onto the bench seat at the kitchen table and scrubbed her face, and said, "I rue the day I ever met that pathetic excuse for a human being," she said softly, painfully. "My father is a good man."

"I'm not saying he isn't. All I'm saying is that I'm not handing you over to Max to be killed."

"Fine," she whispered. "But you better have a plan that saves my father."

"I get that," he said. "We just need time."

"We need to go home now," she said. "My leg is fine. I rested all day yesterday again, and that's all the rest it'll get." The two men looked at her, and she shook her head. "Don't," she said. "Don't even start. We go home to Florida today. You tell his kidnapper, undoubtedly my ex or someone in his employ, that I'm on the way. That's all Max wants. It's just me that he wants. Well—and his precious docs."

"But he's not getting you," Killian snapped.

"He has to," she argued.

"No." Killian shook his head slowly but firmly. "Not what your father hired us for."

She burst into tears. She wanted to rail at him; she wanted to hit him and force him to do this. She understood, at the same time, that—if their positions were reversed—she would probably do the same thing as he was doing now. But it wasn't fair; it wasn't fair at all. Her father needed so much more than this, and he deserved a good life. "He's a good man," she said. "It's not fair."

"It might not be fair," he said, "but that's just what it is."

She sat here slumped over, tears pouring down her face, until she scrubbed her face and said, "Get me home. You'll have done your job, and you are off the hook."

"It's not that easy," he said.

"It is exactly that easy," she said in a hard tone. "I don't need your services anymore. I can get home on my own."

"No," he said. "Not happening."

She glared at him. "Why?"

"Your father hired us to keep you safe," he said. "How do you think that'll go over if we let you get hurt to save him?"

She stared at him for a long moment and then slowly sagged in place. "We have to do something," she wailed.

"And we will," he said. "Remember, Stacey. This is what we do."

She took a long deep breath, exhaled loudly, and said, "Then we need to eat, so we can leave afterward."

"Are you sure you're ready?"

"It doesn't matter," she said. "You and I both know that Dad's out of time."

Just then Killian's phone rang again. He answered it. "Yes? Okay, good," he said. "We'll be on the next set of flights. Give us two hours to get out of here." He checked his watch, listened to something else, and then said, "That's fine. We'll make it." When he hung up the phone, he said, "Well, you're getting your wish. We're heading home today."

She beamed and bounced her feet, only to stop and shudder in pain.

He nodded. "And you'll pay the price," he said seriously.

"*I* can pay it," she said. "I'm strong, and I'm young. My father is neither of those."

"I get it," he said. "Your father's kidnapper has issued orders."

"Of course he has," she said bitterly. "And I am to be delivered into his grasp, I presume?"

"Something like that," he said. "But first, we have to get you back to the States."

"I know." She walked slowly back to where the cooked

bacon was, scooped up a handful, and started munching.

"Hey, let me finish that," he said, as he walked back over. "While I do this, you go pack."

"Nothing to pack," she said.

"Well, there is, but we don't have a whole lot of time, before we'll be gone."

She nodded but ignored him. Mostly because she was processing all this, was frozen, couldn't really do anything right now. But she did notice that Hatch got up quickly, packed up their laptops and paperwork, separated things out, and then disappeared into the bedrooms. "He's coming too, isn't he?"

"Yes, we're both going," he said. "Why?"

"I don't know," she said. "I just, it feels so disjointed and weird right now."

"Everything that's happened to you is kind of on the weird side," he said, with a note of humor. "Make sure you have your medicine where you can get to it. Your antibiotics and the painkillers. It'll be a rough journey."

"It shouldn't be that bad," she said.

He gave her a rueful smile. "Going home fast," he said, "doesn't mean it'll be comfortable."

She nodded. "I'm not sure what you mean by that, but I'll prepare myself for anything, as long as I get to Dad."

"Well, it won't matter how much you prepare," he said, "this flight won't be the same as any of your others. Now sit, and let's eat."

⚓

A QUICK TWO hours later, he secured her buckle in the military cargo plane, near the back, where a few jumper seats were. He was right beside her, and Hatch was on the other side. Their bags had been strapped in too. He'd warned her it wouldn't be terribly comfortable, and she'd been surprised when they didn't go through the same security that she would have expected on a commercial flight. But the main thing was that they were on a US military base and heading home as soon as they could.

But they were in for a couple long hard flights.

They were heading from Canada to Seattle and then making a couple more stops on the way to Florida, to her dad's house. And it would be a full day.

Killian murmured and said, "It'll be a long flight. You might as well try to close your eyes."

Her eyes were already bloodshot from worry and fear over her father, which Killian understood, but it wouldn't help if she crashed.

"Remember," he said. "You need your strength for what is to come. You're no help if you're not capable of doing what we need you to do."

She nodded ever-so-slowly and whispered, "I'm trying."

"I know you are, but you have to listen to me and try to rest as much as you can."

Immediately she closed her eyes. He reached over and popped the headset on her ears, so that it would muffle any loud noises. This cargo plane would get even louder, depending on what kind of turbulence they encountered. The best thing she could do was sleep, if she could.

He sat back, texting as much as he could to get through to the bosses, as they sat here, figuring out a plan.

As soon as she nodded off, he unbuckled, walked to Hatch, sat down, and asked, "Any ideas? We need a plan."

"Good luck with that," he said.

"Until we get any orders or further intel, we don't have anything to go on."

"It's always that way, isn't it?" Hatch said. "It's a pain in the ass, really."

"I'm tired of these guys jerking our chains."

"Well, I don't understand what happened to the two agents protecting her father," Hatch said.

"I asked for details, and all I got was that neither of the men were in any condition to talk."

"If Max left them alive, I'll take that as a good thing," Hatch said. "Because this asshole doesn't like to leave anybody talking, I don't think."

"I feel sorry for the old guy. This has got to be a dad's worst nightmare. Not only is his daughter not safe but he'll be used to get her back to Max, and her father knows his daughter well enough that she would do anything to save him."

"And we can't let her," he said quietly.

"I know," Killian murmured.

"But how will you convince her of that?"

"There is no convincing her. She doesn't get it. She's a distraught daughter worried about her father. And she can hate me all she wants, but I can't give her over to Max in these circumstances."

"And the guilt will eat at her for the rest of her life."

"I know. I do know that," Killian said. "And that's not terribly nice for me either. I don't want to live with that on my conscience, but I would never let her sacrifice her own life to save his."

"No," Hatch said. "And it's even harder because she's sweet on you."

"I don't know about that, but this deal is likely to kill

that off in a heartbeat," he said, his tone harsh.

"Maybe not," he said. "She knows that you're doing everything you can to help both her and her dad."

"But what she wants, and what I want, will be very different things," Killian said. "But my will must prevail."

"I know, but we have to trust that something will work out."

"I get it. I'm just not too sure how any of it'll go."

CHAPTER 8

STACEY THOUGHT THAT the cargo plane wouldn't be that bad, but it was terrible. She struggled with the noise; she struggled with the landing. Everything was just so uncomfortable. By the time they finally landed in Seattle, she was tired and stressed and in more pain again. She constantly clung to Killian's side, and that bothered her too.

Finally he asked her, "What's the matter?"

She shrugged. "I used to be an independent woman," she said. "Now I find myself looking for boogeymen around every corner, and I don't like it. That's not who I am. Not who I want to be."

"But to be extra cautious is the smart thing to do right now," he said. "Let's not forget that you've been attacked twice, and your father is being held by a sadistic bastard who's looking to have you back in his clutches."

"*Great*," she said. "Thanks. That really helps a lot."

Hatch laughed out loud in delight at her retort, while Killian smiled gently, wrapped his arm around her shoulders, and tucked her up close. "We're doing what we can to keep you both safe."

She nodded, as the guys helped her off the plane, and she took a slow deep breath of fresh air. "So where to?"

"The next leg is to Redding, California," Hatch said. "We need to get you to the safe-deposit box and to the material that you stole."

She winced. "You know? When you put it that way, it's kind of easy to see why Max is pissed off at me."

"He's pissed off because you took proof of his illegal activities," he said. "Simple as that."

"Maybe," she said.

"We leave in forty minutes," Killian said, "so walk around a bit, stretch your legs."

She nodded, did what she could to loosen up her legs, without loosening up her stitches. Finally in California and freed of yet another cargo plane, she was happy to walk again, even if sore. In the rental car, she gave the guys directions to the bank. Once there, she asked the teller for access to her box. It took a few minutes of waiting before somebody came and led her and Killian into the private safe-deposit box access area.

Left alone now, she asked, "Where's Hatch?"

"Checking for Max's friends. Trying to look like he's not with us," he said. "Just so we have a little more distance between us."

"Is that safe?"

"We have our team watching via satellite and any street cams, so it gives Hatch the freedom to move around a little bit more," he said. "Having someone on the ground to watch our backs is good, yet he's not right beside us. So he's less likely to become a target himself."

"Oh, good," she said instantly. "The last thing I want is anybody else to be a target."

"A little late for that," he said quietly.

"I know, and that makes me feel even worse," she said.

"Enough of that. It serves no purpose," he said. "Open this thing up, and let's get going."

She nodded and got into it and handed him the flash drive on top.

"Why did you take this? What's on it?"

She shrugged. "No idea. It was on his desk, so I took it too."

He shook his head. "Jesus, no wonder he's pissed."

"Here's the ledger too," she said, pulling out the big book. Then she helped him take a photo of every page, before slipping the large ledger into the tote bag she carried like an oversize purse.

Closing the safe-deposit box, they returned to the front part of the bank, where she thanked the teller.

As they walked outside and got into the rental car, she said, "I don't even know what's on the memory stick. I didn't even take time to look."

"Maybe that's to your benefit," he said. "As soon as we get back to the plane, on the flight, I'll copy everything, so we've got a backup."

"You should do it before we leave," she said. "The internet will be terrible in the air."

"I know."

Safely back at the cargo plane, they were allowed to board, and he sat in the back and quickly uploaded the contents of the flash drive and sent it all off to Jerricho. Then Killian sent all the photographs of the ledger pages he had taken, with a message explaining where they had gotten it all from. As soon as he was done, he noted Hatch, sitting on the far side, ignoring them.

"He does that role really well, doesn't he?"

"Hey, when you use these transport planes," he said, "you could be with anybody. You really have no idea who else is on board."

"I guess."

Killian asked, "What's the matter? You want to go sit with him?"

She shook her head. "Nope, no offense to him, but I'd much rather be with you."

"Why is that?" he asked in surprise.

"Because I like you," she said. "I feel safe here."

"Good," he said. "At least you understand that I won't hurt you."

"Well, it'll take me a while to really trust at that level," she said sadly, "but you don't seem like the kind of a guy who would hurt women."

"So, because you've made one bad decision, you're afraid you have permanent bad judgment, and you'll make another—or what?"

She looked at him and nodded. "That's exactly right. I don't want to be a fool all over again."

"Are you worried about being a fool or about making a decision that's so wrong that you'll get hurt again?"

"See? That's even more to the point," she said. "I just don't want to dwell on the pain I went through."

"You shouldn't have to," he said quietly. "Look. There's no pressure to do anything or to make any big decisions about your future. How about just taking every day from now on for what it is and to make it as good as it can be. That will help."

"Maybe," she said. "I'm just not so sure where any of this will go."

"Well, let's hope it will lead to a whole new life, just for you."

"As long as it includes my father at my side, that's fine," she said.

He shook his head. "I don't know anything about your father, your father's health, or any of the other circumstances that he might be dealing with," he said. "So I can't guarantee that for you at all. Obviously that what's we hope for, but you know better than anybody just what this man Max is like."

She nodded grimly. "He is an asshole, and he thrives on causing pain."

"Exactly," he said, "so just know that we're are doing the best we can for you and for your father."

"I guess I have no choice." With a long cleansing exhale, she gave herself a little shake and changed the subject. Looking at Killian, she asked, "So what will you do after all this is over?"

"Probably head back home and wait for the next job," he said cheerfully.

"No plans to ever get married, have a family, or have what other people call a normal life?"

"Well, that's in the plans—at some point in time," he said. "Somewhere *out in the future* is what I've always thought."

She laughed. "I was the same way," she said. "I was just too busy, and then all of a sudden I met him, and it seemed like he was the one, so I just jumped in with both feet."

"Nothing wrong with that," he reminded her.

"Have you ever been married?" she asked.

"No," he said. "Never, not even close."

"Ah, are you the shy type, afraid of commitment?"

"I don't think so," he said. "I was just waiting for a person who would make me change my mind."

"And you still haven't met her?"

"No," he said. "Well, maybe. What do I know?"

She looked at him sideways. "Well, I know it's not me," she said, "because I'm no bargain at all."

"How do you figure that?"

"Well, I'll try not to worry, but everything is just so messed up now."

He smiled at her and said, "You're not a bad deal or somehow tainted, so just stop it."

"I don't know," she said. "When you feel like such a failure, it's hard to see anything positive."

"You'll get past that too," he said firmly.

She grinned at him. "Well, in that case," she said, "do you want to go out for coffee or something, when this is over?"

He looked at her in surprise and started to laugh.

She frowned immediately. "I didn't mean it as a joke."

He struggled to stop his laughter, but joy filled his heart. "I'm not laughing at you," he said. "I'm laughing at how quickly you turn from one subject to another. You're like a chess player, moves ahead of the rest."

"I've always been lightning fast in my thinking," she murmured. "But that's still not an answer."

"*Yes.* The answer is yes. I would absolutely love to," he said. She looked at him in surprise, and he stared at her and asked, "What? You weren't expecting that for an answer?"

She shook her head. "No, I really wasn't."

"Why not?" he asked curiously.

She shrugged. "Because I guess I see myself as damaged, not what anybody else will want now."

"Well, you can park that idea," he said. "You're dynamite to be around. You're a very sexy, healthy, beautiful woman, and your heart is in the right place."

"Is it though?" she whispered.

"Yes," he said. "So enough of that."

She slowly nodded. "Okay, … a really nice coffee spot that I love is just a few minutes from the beach in Florida where Dad lives, so I often pick up a coffee there, then go sit by the water."

"That sounds lovely," he said. "I have to admit that I'm more of a take-out-coffee guy, going for a walk with it, than to sit in a coffee shop and talk for hours."

"All that inaction would kill you, wouldn't it?"

He grinned. "It's not that so much, as I just really like being outdoors. I'm a more of a doer in life, than a sitter."

"The world needs sitters too," she said.

"Absolutely it does," he murmured. "But you know that, if you're not the kind of person who can sit there quietly and do nothing, it's almost a punishment."

They spoke for a little bit longer, and then she nodded. "I'm getting tired again, but I'm a little scared of nodding off. That last plane was so uncomfortable. I got a kink in my neck from it."

He said, "Here. Use my shoulder."

She looked at him and said, "That might just be a little too dangerous."

"Why is that?" he asked.

"Because I could probably get really comfy, and I don't really want to lean on anybody at this point in time in my life."

"You have to sometimes, in life," he said. "And, if there was ever a time to lean on somebody, it's right now. We're here to help. We're safe, and we're people you can absolutely trust. So close your eyes, relax, and get some rest."

And she did just that.

KILLIAN SAW HATCH grinning from ear to ear. Rolling his eyes, Killian just ignored his buddy. Two other enlisted men were in the front of the cargo plane, on the other side. Killian had heard them talking, but, as long as Hatch was here, keeping watch, it was fine.

Killian checked his phone, but nothing was back from the team. He sent out a message, looking for an update on the father, looking for an update on any of the information they'd requested. Some of it was slow to come, but the team had found two other kidnapping cases in British Columbia, matching a similar pattern as the guy who had kidnapped Stacey the second time, including the leg injuries. It still blew Killian away that somebody would take advantage of a woman suffering so badly. But now, with all these cases lining up, it had caught the interest of the RCMP, and they were also looking into some of the cases farther up the coastline.

Which was good.

They needed to hear back from Alaska too, from the governor of the other nearby territories as well. And, with everybody lined up, there should be an all-points bulletin out for this guy.

The trouble was, nobody really had a good description. All of the women were being interviewed again, looking for some description, and sketches were being made and called into play. To think that somebody had done this for so long was ludicrous. But it made Killian feel a lot better to think the authorities were getting around to this guy.

He hadn't told Stacey yet that they were stopping in Texas. Killian had an itch to get into Max's house.

After the landing, he had to wake her up as they taxied toward the deplaning area. She yawned, looked at him, and stretched, saying, "Well, that went better than I thought."

"See? Leaning on someone is good," he teased.

She smiled. "You're a nice man."

"Ouch."

She looked at him in surprise.

"For a guy, that's not exactly a compliment."

"No," she said, frowning. "Being nice is a huge compliment."

"Doesn't sound that great to me," he grumbled.

"Why? Because you want to hear that you're sexy and cute and all the rest of that?"

"Everybody wants to hear that," he said.

She started to laugh. "I can't imagine that you have a small ego," she said. "You have an enormous ability to handle stress, dangerous situations, rescues, and things like that, in a way that I've never seen in anybody else. So you're a very special person."

"Well, I try to be. And someone with this skill set," he said, "is custom made specifically for these situations."

"See? I didn't even realize people out there did this," she murmured. "I would have felt a whole lot better the whole time I was being held hostage if I had thought there was any hope of somebody being out there, looking for me."

"Well, in this case, you still needed somebody who cared for you," he said. "Cared enough to make that phone call."

"And Dad does. Which is why I have to make sure that we get him back safe."

"We're on it, remember?"

She nodded.

"And, by the way, we found several more cases, looking

like your second kidnapper."

She shook her head. "That bastard needs to pay for his crimes," she said. "Somebody needs to slice his legs wide open and leave him for the rats."

"There's the spirit," he said. "Better to feel anger than to feel fear around people like him and Max."

She looked up, smiled, and gave him a big hug. "I don't know what it is about you," she said, "but I seem to be feeling better and better all the time."

"It's because you got some rest and relaxed a bit and let that leg of yours heal."

"It's coming along," she said.

"Maybe, but it's still got a long way to go," he said.

"Well, it'll just have to wait," she said. "You can argue with me about that when my father is safe."

"Well, I won't be arguing with you then either," he said. "I'll have you tucked into bed, on strict bed rest."

"Are you coming to bed with me too?" she teased.

He looked at her in surprise.

She flashed him a smile and said, "Of all the things that I've learned with this series of events is that you don't know from one day to the next just what the hell's coming your way. So, if this is something I want, I should probably ask for it."

"You know what? I'm not against the idea," he said. "Believe me. I'm not. I just want to make sure that it's got nothing to do with gratitude or something along those lines."

CHAPTER 9

"OH BOY," STACEY said. "I get how you wouldn't want a personal relationship based on gratitude in your world. I hadn't even considered it though, since that's not how I see you."

"Good, because I'm not any kind of knight in shining armor."

"Absolutely," she said firmly. "How about my shiny knight in armor instead? And I hope you stay that way."

"Don't put me on a pedestal," he said seriously. "It's too hard to stay up there."

She looked at him with genuine surprise, then nodded. "You're right, and I didn't mean to make you feel like I wasn't grounded in reality here," she said. "I'm just, you know, if I say I'm grateful, then you'll think it's a matter of gratitude all over again."

"Well, it is," he said.

"It is, and it isn't. I can be grateful for all you've done, yet still have an interest in you on a completely different level. Of course, other factors should be considered also—the pain, fear, head injury, adrenaline, guilt. All of that weighs in somehow as well."

"Good," he said. "In that case, hold that thought."

"What thought was that?" she asked in confusion.

He laughed and said, "Don't tell me that you've already

forgotten? You know—your invitation, to, uh, go to bed."

"Oh that," she said and then burst out laughing. "I haven't forgotten. The offer still stands."

"And I'll take you up on it," he said, "but not until all this is over."

"That works for me too," she said. "Maybe we should go away for a few days and really get to know each other, without all this in the way."

"Hey, I'm all for that," he said. "A few days somewhere warm, with a beach, where that leg can get lots of sunshine."

"I'm good with that too. I have access to a cabin close to Redding," she said. "So, if that appeals?"

"Absolutely," he said. "How about a weekend?"

"How about a week?" she said.

"Even better."

"Okay, so if you two are done arranging your futures or whatever," Hatch said, with a teasing glint in his eye, "do you think we could get at it?"

She glared at him. "We weren't ignoring where we are."

"No, of course not," Hatch said, chuckling. "But all of us just heard you make arrangements for a week away. We even know where you're going."

She flushed. "I guess we weren't exactly keeping things private, were we?"

"It's all good," he said cheerfully. "I've been telling Killian that he should be doing just what you did."

"What did I do?"

"Made a move and hooked yourselves up together," he said. "I told him that he should have done that a while ago."

"Really?" she said in delight.

"Yep. It's obvious to me that this is a relationship that needs to be explored."

"Well, I think you're right," she said. "I just hadn't really seen it, until I woke up this last time."

"Right," Killian said, with a roll of his eyes. "How the hell does that work?"

"I don't know," she said, facing him. "Just, when I woke up, I saw the tilt of your lips and the shape of your profile, and suddenly I felt like I was home or something. I don't know how to explain it."

"No, I get it," Killian said quietly. "It's just one of those things."

"It is, indeed. And it feels good. I'd like to see where it goes."

"Me too."

With that, Hatch said, "Hello, I'm still here."

She grinned at him. "Yep, and that makes it even more special."

He rolled his eyes and said, "Okay, that's … Let's go." He followed them off the cargo plane, heading toward some SUVs parked nearby.

"I thought we're going in different vehicles?"

"We are," Hatch said. "Killian is driving you guys in that one, and I'm taking this one." With a casual wave, Hatch lifted his hand and hopped into the driver's seat.

She looked over at Killian, as they kept walking. "Seriously, he's leaving us?"

"He will follow us," he said. "Just on a different avenue." He pointed at the vehicle up ahead. "This is ours."

"I don't know how you guys keep all this stuff straight," she confessed.

"It's not that hard, but it's not easy either. It just takes practice, and I've been doing this a long time."

"How long?"

And that started off a stream of questions that she couldn't seem to stop asking.

Finally he laughed and said, "Hold on. I need to pay attention here. We're coming up on where we want to go."

At that, she stopped, looked at him, and asked, "Where's that?"

He smiled and said, "A rendezvous point for your father."

She gasped. "Already?" Just that quickly, the color drained from her face.

"Yep, already."

"Why didn't you tell me?"

"Because there's no way to make it easy," he said. "This is what we're facing right now."

"Okay," she said, but her voice was faint.

"Don't pass out on me now," he said.

She shook her head and replied, "Never. I wouldn't give that bastard the satisfaction."

"Well, hopefully you won't have to see him or deal with him," he said. "We have several other men in play this time around."

"Good," she said. "I feel better, knowing that we're not going into this alone."

"Nope, we're not," he said. "I have to ensure we have as much going for us as we can."

"Got it," she said, as she took a deep breath. "As long as my father is still alive."

"He is, as far as we know, and that's what we must hang on to."

"Got it," she said. "Then let's go. Let's go rescue my dad."

⚓

IF ONLY IT were that easy. It sounded good, but, at the same time, Killian and Hatch and the team were painfully aware of a few hiccups. And one was that there was a good chance her father was already gone.

Killian parked the SUV and got out, coming around to open her door. She stood beside him and now faced Killian. "What's the plan?" Meanwhile Hatch jogged off on his own. She frowned at that.

"We need more than a plan to just hand you over," he said. "I don't trust that Max is coming alone with your father."

"Not in any way, shape, or form," she said quietly. "I never thought he was the kind to get his hands dirty, until he started beating me," she said. "And then I realized he just saved the best ones for himself."

"Meaning that, he will be there in person when we supposedly hand you over?"

"Absolutely, and then he'll take me off someplace else, where he can take his time."

"Well, that won't happen," Killian said. He saw the hope, and the fear, warring in her expression. He reached over with a muffled exclamation and pulled her into his arms and just held her. "I promise."

She nodded, but he could tell she didn't believe him. She stepped back a moment, looked up at him, and said, "I know that's what you believe," she said. "But, the truth of the matter is, sometimes things happen out of our control, and there's absolutely nothing we can do about it."

"That's true, but an awful lot that we can do *is* within our control," he murmured. "And that's what I'll focus on."

She sighed. "Do we have any more details?"

"Yes," Killian said, lifting his phone. "Apparently a wooded area is about ten miles from here," he said. "I'll bring it up on the GPS. Hunting…"

"Huntington Woods," she said instantly.

He glanced at her and nodded. "You know it?"

"I do. We're in Texas? I thought we were going to Dad's house in Florida?"

Killian shook his head. "Max brought your father here, on Max's home turf."

"Figures. My husband and I used to walk there all the time. It's fairly close to his house, and the woods are wild looking, with lots of trails and pathways through the brush. One time we saw coyotes and a few other critters. So it's definitely got that wilderness edge to it."

"What else can you tell me about it?"

"Not a whole lot. Not really anything to tell," she admitted. "Let me think though." Closing her eyes, she said, "There's an entrance off Parkway Avenue, with a little bit of a parking lot, room for maybe three vehicles," she said, keeping her eyes closed. "As you walk in, a sign with a direction arrow points out the path." Mentally, it looked like she was walking forward, as she said, "When we get to the far side of the path, there is another entrance and another exit, and it goes to Wilbur Street on the other side. Then, as you come back and around, it leads you up to Huntington Woods again."

"Okay," he said. "Good job. So three entrances and exits. Any idea how big the wooded area is?"

Her eyes flew open. "I'm terrible with size and distance," she said apologetically.

"Okay, don't even think about that. Let's look at it differently. How long does it take you to walk it?"

"If we go at a stroll all the way around, it's about forty-five minutes," she said, as she tilted her head, thinking about it. "If we get angry and have a fight on the way, it takes about two-thirds of that time," she said. "A creek runs through it, with a little bridge over it. Every once in a while, ducks are there. I always like to stop and enjoy the birds and various wildlife," she said.

"Okay, that's helpful," he said. "Is it heavily wooded, as in blocking out the sunlight, or is it thinly treed, with a little bit of cedar or a little bit of, you know, evergreen here and there?"

"Thick," she said immediately. "It's often very hard to find your way through it because it can be quite dark. If you don't stay on the path, I imagine it would be very easy to get lost, but the park's not that big. So you could walk from one side to the other, without any trouble, and eventually find your way out."

"So, in other words, it'll be full of natural hiding places."

Her mouth formed an O, as she looked at him and then nodded. "Yes," she said. "Plus I have some memories there that are likely to throw me off."

"Why is that?"

"Max hit me there once and chased me, and when he, … when I finally collapsed, he acted like I had been the one completely out of control. Like he was wondering what was wrong with me, why had I taken off."

"You said he hit you?"

"Well, I thought so at the time, but then he had me convinced that it was a limb that came out and smacked me across the jaw. That I jumped to conclusions and overreacted when I bounded to my feet and bolted," she said. "Just call it a Neanderthal reflex. It wasn't until later, another time that he was punching me, that he'd admitted that it wasn't a branch and that he had hit me that day and what an idiot I was for being so gullible as to believe him. Besides, how could I have not seen him punch me right in the face?"

"He's quite the bastard, isn't he?"

"He was very much into mind games," she said quietly. "At one point in time, you're not even sure what is a game and what isn't."

"It's hard to discern the truth because you've been tangled up listening to him go back and forth with his lies for so long that you believed him, at least partially. And that's pretty normal. It's also how abusers groom their victims, so stop taking that on yourself."

"Anyway," she said, "I'm sure that's why he chose that location deliberately. Just to mess with my head."

"So, if we were to look at that, do you think there's any hidden meaning?"

"Sure," she said. "Do I think that he's likely to be playing another mind game? Absolutely. What about a shooter in the trees?"

"Well, that's always possible," Killian said. "I just don't know."

"Why wouldn't he? He's not the kind of guy who'll lose," she said.

"But is he this kind of guy who wants the world to find out that he beats up women?"

"Well, his buddy knows absolutely. Did you ever find James?"

"No, but we have people out looking for him."

"If he knows I had anything to do with that bull's-eye on James's back," she said, "Max will be furious."

"On his own behalf or on his friend's?"

"Both," she said. "They're very close. He seems very protective of James Dean, and I think they both have a kindred mind-set. I've never seen James with a girlfriend, and I think that's because he's the kind of guy who … likes to beat them up. And probably overnighters only."

"Interesting."

"Yet he has *friends*. Don't ever doubt that."

"Sure, but I can't imagine that he has too many, with that mind-set," Killian said. "He doesn't need anybody else. He's already a sadist, and the fact that the sadist has found Max, another friend of the same ilk," he said, "well, that's bad news for the world. They don't need anybody else. They'll feed off of each other and each other's deeds. So you would just likely be a starting point."

"Oh," she said, "I'm not even sure about a *starting* point."

"Mary, right. You said he'd been married before."

She nodded slowly. "Yes, I did. We might need to look into what happened to her."

"We're already waiting for information on that," he said quietly.

"I really was a fool, wasn't I?"

"You were blinded by love and believed what was in front of you," he said. "That isn't what makes you a fool."

"Oh, you mean something else does?" she said in exasperation.

He burst out laughing.

She shook her head. "How can we be laughing at a time like this?"

"Because it's good for the soul," he said. "You have to relax and let some things happen, the way they have to happen."

"None of that makes any sense to me," she said.

"I get that." Just then, his phone rang. He answered Hatch's call and put it on speaker.

"We have two men in position," Hatch said.

"Where?"

"Huntington Woods," Hatch replied.

She nodded. "Let's go then," she said. "No time like the present, and I don't know how much time my father has."

Both men were silent for a hair too long, and she was on to them. "You don't think he's alive, do you?" she asked.

"I think he is alive," Killian said, with that note of surety because he really did believe it.

She looked at him in surprise. "So what was that silence for?"

"We don't think he'll stay that way for long," Hatch said, then ended the call.

CHAPTER 10

STACEY'S HEART POUNDED as Killian drove her toward Huntington Woods. Something about Hatch's voice, that note of finality in what he had said, made her want to throw up. Especially since she knew Killian felt the same way. Yet she wanted to get on with it, to get her husband's throat in her hands, and to squeeze the life out of him for what he had done to her and now her father. But, for her father, she felt terror and worried that he had been taken to the point where he could never recover. Even mentally, she knew it would be hard for him, no matter what happened physically.

But she got the impression from Killian that Dad was alive, probably long enough for her to see him, she surmised, then wouldn't survive long past the meeting. And that, she vowed fiercely, would not happen. Her father's only mistake had been the same one that she had made: to trust this terrible man. And, while the fact that Dad hadn't believed her was terribly hurtful, no way she could hold her father's earlier beliefs against him. It was just so far out of his comprehension to think that anyone could be as evil as her husband Max had turned out to be. No way for Dad to make any sense of it.

Killian looked at her and asked, "Is the divorce final?"

"No," she said. "Max wouldn't sign the papers."

"Of course not."

"What do you mean?"

"Because, when he signs the papers, they have to be filed on record, and people would know," he said. "I suspect that would be something he wouldn't want people to have any clue about."

"Why would he care?" she said. "As far as he's concerned, I'm the reason the marriage didn't work."

"Of course, because otherwise he'd be responsible, and that won't work for him."

She shrugged. "I don't care who's responsible. The guy's a psychopath, and I just wanted out."

He laughed. "And I get that. I just wondered if any paperwork was involved."

"No, not yet," she said. "And I don't … don't know that it'll ever happen."

"It will," he said. "Or something will anyway."

She wasn't sure what that meant and decided, after a moment's contemplation, that she didn't want to know either. The closer they got to Huntington Woods, the more her nerves kicked in. She was not quite hyperventilating, but almost.

He glanced at her and said, "It's okay. Calm down."

"It's not okay," she said, giving him a look. "You don't understand what he's like."

"No, but I've met plenty like him," he said.

Just then Killian pulled off-road and drove into the woods themselves.

She gasped, as branches hit the side of the SUV and bounced off the vehicle. "What are you doing?" she cried out.

"We're going in a different way," he said. "No way we'll

approach the enemy in the front entrance."

"And you don't think he'll expect this?"

"Did you?"

She stopped, looked at him, and shook her head. "Can you hide the vehicle well enough?"

"Well, that's the hope," he said. "We mapped this out a while ago."

"Like when?"

"At least two hours ago," he said.

She rolled her eyes at that, but inwardly she was more than delighted to have some kind of a plan that wouldn't start off with a full-on confrontation. "Any chance you can go in and kill Max before we get to the part about having to meet him?"

"Well, we need to meet him," he said.

"We don't have to," she said, shaking her head. "We could just shoot him or incapacitate him, then grab my father and run."

"We aren't running," he said quietly. "Once you do that, it never ends."

She stared at him and then slowly nodded because, of course, he was right. As soon as she had run, she had no way to go back, no way to face what she had left behind, because she was too terrified of what he would do to her. And that had given him the upper hand. "So what's the plan then?"

"You'll stay here with Hatch," he said.

She glared at him.

"You'll stay here with Hatch until I get a chance to see the lay of the land," he explained. "You must show up anyway because he'll never talk to us, or trust us, unless you're there."

"You'll have to watch for James Dean too," she said.

"Oh, I will," he said. "Not to worry." He pushed open his door, slipped outside, then leaned over the seat and looked at her and said, "Stay here." He melted into the trees so fast that he was here one second and then gone.

Her jaw dropped. "Wait! I thought you said … Hatch would be here," her voice dropping, realizing she was talking to thin air.

"I'm right here," Hatch said, as she jumped.

"Jesus, don't do that! Where did you come from?" she snapped at him. "What's going on?"

"Killian's gone to check out our surroundings," Hatch said.

"Is that safe?" Then she quickly added, "No, of course it's not safe." Hating herself for even asking such a stupid question.

"Maybe not safe," he said, "but we have two more men we're in contact with, and they've already told us exactly where several people are standing near a bench."

"My father?"

"Well, we're hoping so. One of them is definitely smaller and hunched over."

At that, she turned to stare at him. "My father is fairly tall," she said, striving for control. "He's at least five-eleven, and he's very lean."

"So, like a string bean?"

"Yes," she said. "And the only way he'd be hunched over is if he was hurt."

"You need to accept the fact that he is hurt. Just as your husband hurt you, he has hurt your father."

Tears came to her eyes at the blatant truth and the harshness of his words.

"I'm not trying to upset you," Hatch said. "But I can't

have you overreacting out here, if things go to pot. I need you calm, controlled, and available to do whatever we need to do to save your father."

"Okay, that's why I'm here," she said faintly. "I understand."

"Good. Now we'll just wait here until there's some information."

"Don't you feel like a bit of a sitting duck here?"

"Not at the moment," he said, "but, as soon as I get any word that we're in danger or in trouble, well, then that's a different story, and we'll be out of here and gone."

"With the vehicle or without?"

"Probably without."

"Then I'm starting to feel like we're already pinched in the wrong spot."

He frowned at her. "What do you mean?"

"It *feels*," she said, emphasizing the word, "like we're being watched."

He raised an eyebrow. "You know what? You could be right," he said. He slipped open his door and asked, "How do you feel about running?"

"I don't like it at all," she said. "But somebody, … somebody out there knows we're here."

"Good," he said, his door still open. "I'll come and open up your door, and I want you to duck as soon as I do."

"Fine," she said. "But I don't know that we'll get anywhere."

"You saw how Killian disappeared?"

She nodded. "Yes."

"That's how we'll disappear."

"But I'm not very good at moving like that in the forest," she said. "And my leg is hardly strong. It's also broad daylight. How the hell does that work?"

"It also means that Max doesn't give a damn about being seen because he's not expecting anybody to be here."

"I don't know why he wouldn't. It's a public park."

"Because he's blocked off the road, saying a sinkhole is an issue, and everybody has to stay back."

"Jesus," she said, staring at Hatch. "A sinkhole opened up not too far from here one time, so people would believe it."

"Exactly," he said. "So basically he has his hunting ground all prepared. The stage is set, and he is just waiting for all the players to arrive."

"But, if somebody is watching us," she said, "then they would have seen Killian leave and you arrive."

"Not necessarily," he said, "but we'll count on that as being a fact, yes."

"Jesus," she said. "Can't we just go now?" An overriding sense of panic filled her.

"I'm not sure we can count on your leg to get you very far."

"I know," she whispered. "Jesus." And the panic started to overwhelm her. She tried hard to stay calm, but it wasn't working. "Maybe we should drive out of here."

"Maybe," he said, "but that would mean leaving Killian behind."

"We can't do that," she said immediately.

"I didn't think we would," he said, smiling. "And I'm happy you agree." He pulled out a handgun from behind him and said, "I want you to keep your door unlocked and you to lie down because you can't move anyway."

"I can move somewhat," she said, but, as she looked at the terrain, she winced.

"Yeah, you would, and, if you needed to, you would again," he said. "But why don't we set a trap, instead?"

She looked at him and realized what he meant and said, "And I'm the bait, I suppose."

"You got a better idea?"

"No," she said instantly.

"So, lie down," he said, and, with that, he disappeared himself.

She sat here, her heart in her throat, knowing that somebody not only was watching but had watched as Hatch disappeared into the trees, probably thinking he'd gone to survey the land, leaving her alone. She almost wanted to howl in a hilarious outraged panic but knew that the sound would come across more like she had completely lost it. Such a stillness was outside that, when she heard a stick *snap*, signaling that somebody was approaching, she almost felt a sense of relief, easing the pressure.

When she heard the cock of a gun, she turned slowly to look, and there, facing her, was her husband, Max.

"Well, well, well," he said. "So the chickee has finally come home."

She looked at him steadily and whispered, "What have you done to my father?"

"Well, get out of that car," he said. "I'll take you to him, and then you'll find out."

"And what then?" she asked bitterly.

"Then you two can die together," he said, with a smile she recognized as one that meant he was thoroughly enjoying himself and was happily anticipating what was to come.

She swallowed hard and said, "I'm not alone."

"Oh, I know," he said. "Your buddy is already out of commission."

KILLIAN CREPT THROUGH the trees to where the park bench was, where he had been warned that two people sat there. He checked in with Hatch to see that everything was okay. When Killian didn't get an answer, he waited a bit. His phone vibrated a moment later. He checked swiftly to make sure all was well. It was Hatch, saying he was fine and he was stepping out for a moment. Killian frowned at that but kept on going. He trusted Hatch, trusted his instincts, and trusted that he would do right by Stacey.

Up ahead was the clearing. Instead of going on the path, Killian slipped deeper into the woods. He wanted to check out the immediate surroundings first. From this distance he saw only one person on the bench now. He swore at that. It was a long, lean man, which he presumed was her father. And he was slumped forward. He could be unconscious; hell, he could even be dead, if he'd been propped up properly. The fact of the matter was, he sat there all alone, which meant that whoever had been with him before was loose.

Killian turned and studied the area around him. He knew that the woods were full of predators, not just two of his own men, but Hatch was out there, and whoever else was with Max and Stacey's dad. Killian didn't trust this James Dean guy, and it gave Killian a bad feeling all the way around. He didn't know why James Dean had skin in this game or would have gotten involved to this degree, unless just as a sadists' club of two.

As Killian stood here, studying the layout, an ever-so-slight cough came from the trees to the left. He frowned at that major slip, as whoever this was could be instantly shot dead. As it was, Killian heard a *ping*, followed by a slump, as if somebody landed on the ground. He hoped it wasn't one of his, but it was possible.

His phone vibrated, and there was a message.

One down.

He grinned at that.

Good, he thought. How many others were out here? He and Hatch had come with two more, so if James Dean and Max were both here, two more with the bad guys would make sense too. When his phone vibrated again not five minutes later with a message of a second man down, he started to relax ever-so-slightly.

Then he got a text from Hatch.

She's in danger.

Swearing silently, Killian looked at her father and knew he really had no decision to be made. An older, apparently already injured man in the waning years of his life or his daughter, who the father had paid Killian to protect? He melted backward, racing toward the vehicle. He saw Hatch, ever-so-slightly off to the side, his shot lined up. As Killian stopped, he followed Hatch's line of sight to see another man standing at the car, holding a gun at Stacey's head. Killian looked at the gunman and frowned. It was Max. It didn't bode well that he had come in person.

Max called out to Hatch, "Put your weapon down. Otherwise I'll kill her."

Hatch immediately lowered his weapon and held up his hands.

Max's voice was disgusted. "You guys follow these stupid damn rules, and you're completely useless," he said. "Just look at you." And, with that, he fired on Hatch. Only Hatch was no longer there. Max swore and fired again. "Show yourself. Otherwise I'll kill her."

At that, a shot rang out, and Max slammed against the car. He started to swear, but he'd already lost control of Stacey, as she quickly jumped back into the vehicle and out the other side. Killian could just imagine how that maneuver had hurt her leg, but he was proud of her for making it. He was a little too far away and didn't have a clear shot at Max, but he knew Hatch would handle it.

What Killian needed to do was get Stacey and keep her safe. If she went barreling through the woods like this, she could get lost, and somebody could find her, and it may not be the right somebody. Taking note of her path, Killian quickly slipped around to cut her off, before she got too deep into the forest.

When he grabbed her, she went to scream, but he slapped a hand over her mouth and held her close, whispering, "It's me. Hold on. It's me."

She fought blindly, until his words slowly penetrated into her brain, and then she collapsed against him, sobbing.

He held her head tightly against his shirt, muffling her sobs, as he held her close. "Easy," he whispered. "Easy."

She shuddered and nodded. "Did you find my father?"

He smiled at that because, even when she was distraught, in shock, and injured, she'd remained focused and was only thinking of her father. "I did."

She lifted her gaze.

"I didn't get to him yet. He's sitting on the bench in the center of the park."

She nodded. "Yeah, that's Max's trick." She turned back in the direction of the car. "Do you think he's dead?"

"That I'm not sure," he said. "I wouldn't trust one bullet to take down a psychopath like that, but we'll go in after your father and leave Hatch to handle Max."

"I don't know if it's that easy," she said.

"Well, Hatch will get his shot at Max first. We'll see after that." Slowly moving her along at a pace she could maintain, but trying to keep the noise down, he knew that every step raised more alarms. He whispered, "Maybe you should stay here. I'll go get your father and bring him back."

She stopped, leaning against the tree, and he saw the sweat on her face.

"You won't make it much farther," he said. "If I go pick him up and carry him back here, we can get out to the road on this side."

She looked at him and nodded. "I'm slowing you down," she whispered.

"You are," he said cheerfully. "But that's only part of it." He leaned over and kissed her hard and said, "I'll be back. Stay here, stay quiet, and don't move." And, on that note, he turned and disappeared.

CHAPTER 11

STACEY WAITED IN the eerie afternoon, as directed. The heated atmosphere around her had a stillness and a weightiness that made her cringe. Her stomach was cramping from being knotted so long with pain and anger. And fear. God, the fear, it was crippling. And speaking of crippling, her leg was killing her. Why she'd ever thought she could do any kind of running now was beyond her. Because that leg was just throbbing. She'd had her pain pills earlier, and, of course, they had already worn off with all the exertion.

She sank back a little bit lower against the tree, hoping that nobody could find her. She knew that two of Killian's men were out there, but she didn't know which ones were which and, bad leg or not, wouldn't waste any time trying to figure it out either before darting away.

So many men were out there, but she didn't want anything to do with any of them but one. She wanted Killian to come back, hopefully carrying her father. But since when had her wants ever mattered in this world? It was a world full of psychopaths, people so sick that they thrived on hurting others. She thought back to a comment Killian had made, something about Max not wanting anyone to know he was divorced. Giving it some thought, especially after seeing and hearing Max in the flesh, she realized Killian was probably right.

Max. His pride and ego were something else to behold. He was such a completely different man now compared to the one who she thought she knew. It just made her wonder why and how she had been so blind. Had he been such a great chameleon that she couldn't see it because he hid it so well? There were just no answers, and that part just added to her pain.

Hearing a sound, she froze and ducked down into the trees a little bit lower. She watched one man, his rifle up, slowly circling through the trees, looking for something, probably her, and she wouldn't get saved from a bullet if he found her. Just when she thought maybe it was one of Killian's men, an arm snaked around the gunman's throat, and down he went.

She gasped in horror as she recognized the man still standing.

Jesus, it was James Dean.

He was here too. That murderous killing bastard. But she had absolutely no hope of running away now. At least not from him. She sank as quietly as she could to the ground, out of sight, hoping that something would save her. Just when she thought the crackling noises beside her would overwhelm her, that bullets would riddle her body any second, she heard shouts in the distance and sirens.

Was that a helicopter?

The silence of the woods had been broken by absolute chaos, as a team of something new moved in. She huddled up tight, as James Dean tore off into the darkness of the shadows in the woods. Relieved, she slowly made her way to the man who James had attacked. She wasn't sure who this man down was, but, as she reached a hand to check for a pulse, she noted his neck was broken, and he was gone. In the game of life and death, James Dean had scored and had scored well. Her bitterness grew as she realized that the only thing that had saved her was whatever that new chaos had been.

She heard a shout from behind and turned to see Killian, where she was supposed to have been. She called out, "I'm here."

He made his way slowly through the trees, carrying her father.

She raced toward them with a cry, falling all over her father, and, with relief, her dad turned and looked at her, then whispered, "I'm okay."

She snorted. "You're not okay. You're hurt."

"Yes," he said.

She looked over at Killian to see his hard gaze locked on the body of one of the men from his team. "I'm sorry," she whispered. "It was James Dean. I saw it happen."

"Good to know," he said. "I'll make sure I get retaliation for that."

"Will that help at all?" she asked.

"It won't hurt," he said.

"Maybe," she murmured. "But we already have one dead. Let's not have any more."

"Well, the police are here," he said. "They've picked up two of Max's men, and we have another two bad guys down."

"What about Max and James?"

"I don't know," he said. "I'm also missing Hatch."

She stared at him in shock. "Dear God, no. Please … no."

"Let's get back to the car," he said. "And get your father taken care of."

She led the way back, following his instructions when she went wrong. When, for the third time, he had her change course, she looked at him and glared. "How is it you can tell where you are, when you've never been here before?"

"Because it's what I do," he said simply.

She rolled her eyes but was heartened by the fact that her father had a smile on his face at their banter. She looked at him, feeling the tears in her eyes, but he waved them off with an ever-so-slight shake of his head. "Go on now," he said. "I told you that I'm fine."

It didn't matter what he said on the subject because she didn't really believe him. But she would do whatever she could to get him some help. It was obvious that he was in a great deal of pain, and that needed to stop, right now. Back at the car, Killian called out to her and said, "Hold on. I want to get ahead of you."

She stopped when she saw the car in her view and let him lead the way. She was completely surprised he held a handgun, even as he carried her father, but the fact that he felt danger was still out here scared her.

"Max was here," she said. "He attacked me, and that's when he went after Hatch."

"And I thought Hatch had made it out of this. I watched him evade Max's bullets." His head perked up, as sirens neared them.

She walked behind him, as they slowly moved their way through and around to the vehicle. It was hard to maneuver with so much underbrush and thick sticky pines. She didn't even remember dashing from the vehicle. When they circled back, Killian ever watchful, he slowly lowered her father into the back seat, the two of them talking quietly. She saw her father wince, as he shifted, trying to get more comfortable.

She turned toward Killian and asked, "How bad is it?"

"It's bad," he said, "but he's alive."

She nodded and said, "Max was here, and I know that Hatch shot him."

"I know. I saw it too. Now I need to find Hatch." He had his phone out and sent a quick message. Then he turned and looked at where the footprints were.

She pointed. "Hatch was over there. Max was standing right here. I swear to God, Max should be dead."

"Where did he take the blow? My angle was blocked."

"I thought in the chest," she said, "but now I don't know."

Killian didn't say anything, just nodded and said, "I want you to stay right here. I'm not going far. I'm just checking where we saw Hatch last." And he headed for the position where Hatch had fired at Max.

She called out, "Maybe he went into the center after you."

"Maybe." He turned and looked at her and said, "The cops are coming up the road behind you."

With that, she turned to see other vehicles. Feeling a sense of relief inside, she nodded, and he disappeared into the trees. She heard him looking, but he wasn't calling out, and that made her wonder. When the first cop pulled up off the side of the road, she motioned to him. A hand was lifted, and two men came toward her.

She said, "We need an ambulance for my father." And she pointed out her dad, slumped in the vehicle.

The cop bent beside him, and she heard the two of them talking.

The other one came over and asked, "Are you alone?"

"No," she said. "Killian is looking for his partner, Hatch,

out here."

"I better go help him."

"I wouldn't do that," she said. "Anybody who isn't expected to be out there is likely to get shot." She said it in such a serious tone because she really meant it. The cop looked at her in surprise. She shrugged. "It's craziness out there right now, with two gunmen aiming for all of us."

"Good to know," he said. "I'm calling for an ambulance for your father."

"Thank you," she said sincerely. "He certainly didn't deserve this."

"Nobody ever does," he said. "But I can tell you that, the gunmen out there, they really don't give a shit."

She nodded. "Thank you for not being one of them."

He gave her a gentle smile and said, "Let me go to the pathway, where I can get better reception, and we'll get this show on the road."

The other cop stayed and talked with her father. She worried that the policeman was just trying to keep Dad awake and keep him cognizant. It was almost as if they knew each other. She just smiled when her father gave her a thumbs-up; then she turned her attention back to where Killian had disappeared. She chewed on her bottom lip, hating that sense of something being so very wrong right now. But, of course, it still was. Until she had all the players out of the forest, and her ex and that asshole James Dean were caught, she would never feel free and clear. When a sudden noise came from her right, she immediately backed up against the police officer. But it was Killian, coming out of the bush, carrying somebody.

She raced toward him. "Is that Hatch?"

He nodded. "It is. But Max's body is back there too."

"Jesus," she said. "Is Hatch okay?"

"He's got a bullet high in the shoulder," he said. "And it looks like a blow to the head."

"I'm fine," Hatch said in a slurred voice.

She glared at him. "You're not fine," she said. "What the hell happened? Didn't you shoot Max?"

"I did, and, when I came to check on him," he said, "he grabbed me. We fought and I managed to get free, but somehow he still was coming after me. I shot him again and dropped him. Then I got tackled, from behind."

"And that would have been James Dean," she said. "Like I said, the two are inseparable."

"Well, I got off another shot, and he ran."

"Well, at least we got one," she said, turning to Killian. "So Max's really dead now?"

"He *is* dead," Killian said.

She looked behind him.

He said, "Don't. We're getting Hatch here some attention. Then I'll go back and get James Dean."

"God," she said, sinking down into the driver's seat. "This has just been such a nightmare."

"It is, yet we're getting it closed up nicely."

"Not unless you get James Dean," she murmured.

"That's next," he said. "Remember?"

"I know."

He put Hatch inside the vehicle, while she sat in the driver's seat. The cop talked to both of them.

"Don't you go unconscious on me," she said to Hatch.

"I was unconscious, but now I'm awake." He looked over at the man seated beside him. "You must be her father. Nice to meet you, sir."

Her father nodded ever-so-slowly. "Thank you so

much," he said, "for taking care of my daughter and for coming and rescuing me. I'm so sorry you got hurt."

"I'm fine," he said. "It goes with the job."

"But you're shot," she said.

He gave her a flat stare. "This is not being shot," he said. "It's hardly a nick. This happens on a regular basis."

She just stared at him.

He nodded. "It's a fact of life. We go up against gunfire on a regular basis," he said. "We have to expect to take a bullet or two once in a while."

She took a long slow deep breath and then nodded. "It's just such a foreign thing for me."

"Sure it is, and it should be," Hatch said. "You don't want to be dealing with all this."

"No," she said. "But, if that's what it is, I'll get accustomed to it."

He grinned. "Meaning?"

"We have to catch James Dean," she whispered.

"We will," he said. "Have a little faith."

Just then they heard more sirens coming.

The cop looked over at her, smiled, and said, "The cavalry is coming to take these two back to the hospital."

"Good," she said, turning to glare at Hatch, who was already shaking his head. "No, no, you don't," she said. "You need to get that looked at."

"I'm fine," he said, with a hard look.

"Stop being so macho," she snapped.

At that, Killian stepped back over and laughed. "He will go and get it looked after because it's the only way he can stay on the job." At that, Hatch rolled his eyes and glared out the window. "You'll be back and fighting fit in no time."

"I'm fighting fit now," Hatch said quietly. "And you're

not going anywhere without me."

"You really think we're still in danger?" she asked.

Hatch turned slowly, looked at her, and said, "James Dean is after you, and he won't stop now."

"I was kind of hoping that, with Max dead, then maybe it was all over." She turned and realized that Killian had headed back into the woods. Fear began to prickle at her consciousness, but, minutes later, he returned, carrying the body of her ex-husband. She felt the bile rise in her throat, as the fear boiled over inside her. "I know this makes no sense," she said, "but I'm still terrified, even though I know he's dead."

"Maybe you want to make sure," Hatch suggested. "Just to know that he won't jump up and run."

She frowned, slowly got out, and walked around to the spot where Max was. She reached out a hand and touched him. When he didn't do anything, she wanted to believe that he was gone. At the same time, ... she still wondered. Then Killian pulled back Max's shirt and bared his chest. She saw the open wound on Max's abdomen. "He was wearing a bulletproof vest," she cried out.

"That's how he evaded the first bullet," Killian said quietly. "Sometimes getting hit, even with a vest, will set you back and looks like you've taken a full-on hit. But, since the bullet doesn't penetrate the body, it's more of a shock and easy to get back up from."

She nodded. "Well, this bastard won't be getting up anymore."

He nodded. "No way."

She let out a long low deep breath. "Thank God," she whispered.

Meanwhile, the cops were helping the EMTs move her

dad to the ambulance. She gave him a little wave and a smile.

"I know," Killian said. "Max's death is one ending, but it doesn't exactly answer any of the other questions though."

"Well, the police can rummage through his life and figure it out after this," she said. "I'm just so damn grateful it's over with, as far as it concerns Max."

"And that's a good way to look at it from now on," he said.

"So, how do we find James Dean?"

"The authorities are already looking for him. The woods are being searched, and they'll hunt him down now."

"He's just ... wily," she said. "I don't know which was worse between the two of them, but I know that I'm just grateful Max is out of commission now."

He helped her back into the driver's seat and said, "Hatch won't go on the ambulance if he can get out of it, so I'll take him to the emergency room myself and get that shoulder looked at. We'll get someone to handle Max's body. So scoot over on this side, and we'll drive out of here."

She nodded and moved into the passenger seat, and Killian drove them slowly, staying out of the way of all the other emergency vehicles, with her father now loaded up into the ambulance. They waited until the ambulance pulled out ahead, while her gaze surveyed the woods. "You're sure the woods are being searched?"

"Absolutely," he said. "Why?"

She turned back to the spot where she just felt that sense of being watched, and, as she did, she thought she saw somebody in the woods. "Because he's there," she said quietly, "watching us."

He looked where she pointed and said, "And, by the time I get there, he'll be long gone." But he pulled out his phone and directed searchers to come in their direction.

And, with that, she said, "Even now I don't know for sure if I saw him."

"I promise you. That area will get searched."

"What if he kills somebody?"

"Well, hopefully not," he said. "We should go now." Then he gave her a head nod.

She looked over at him. "What?"

"Look at your leg."

When she looked down, she gasped.

"When did that happen?" he asked.

"I don't know," she said.

"Well, that's another reason we'll go to the hospital," he said. "That leg needs to be looked at."

And, sure enough, she had rivulets of blood flowing down her already injured leg. She sagged back, as the pain hit her. "Why didn't it hurt before?" she murmured.

"It happens that way sometimes. You're still so stressed and in shock that you don't realize how injured you are, until it's pointed out. Once you see it for yourself, it hurts."

"Then why would you point it out?" she cried out at him.

In the back seat, Hatch laughed. "See?" he said. "It's not me who needs to go the hospital. It's you."

"I'm fine," she said, growling back at him.

And that made Hatch laugh even more, as she repeated Hatch's words from earlier back at him.

She sagged against her seat. "Well, aren't we a hell of a pair?"

"Yep," Killian said. "Now I have two of you to look after."

"Like hell," they both snapped at the same time. At that,

they both started to laugh.

Killian grinned and headed off toward the hospital, following the ambulance.

⚓

KILLIAN WAS GRATEFUL that it had ended as well as it had, but he was still pissed that one of the bad guys had gotten away and devasted at the loss of a good man. An odd suspicion popped up in the back of his mind, when he caught the profile of Dean. He wasn't exactly sure what he'd seen and didn't want to bring it up—in case he was completely off—but Killian was racking his memory, trying to match it up. Something was so familiar about what he thought was James Dean's profile.

If it was even him.

And that was frustrating in itself because it was really hard, with the heavy forest lending its own darkness, to get a clear view of anything.

At the hospital, nobody argued with Killian. But Hatch and Stacey were arguing back and forth, amiably, to the point that it was almost a joke. Killian knew Hatch was just trying to keep her positive and upbeat, while he kept his own mind diverted from the pain. And she was probably doing the same thing. In many ways they were alike, and that would probably drive them all crazy. But Killian smiled, as he moved both of them into the hospital emergency area, where they were put into a private room and quickly checked over.

Some advantages came with being part of the Mavericks team, and, man, Killian needed that right now.

Very quickly, Hatch was wheeled out for a CAT scan of

his head and to precisely determine the location of the bullet. By the time he got back, chances were, the bullet would already be out. The surgery might be a little on the rough side, being done in secrecy, without all the typical frills. But it would be done and done fast.

As for Stacey, Killian frowned as he looked at her, her leg still bleeding. "Is that a new gash, or did you rip your stitches?"

She shrugged. "I have no clue and don't even really care. I'm just worried about my father."

"He's here. I'll go get a status update for you." He stepped out and went to talk to the nearest nurse. She gave him the little bit that they knew at this point—that her father was being checked over intensively, and, as yet, they had no definitive answers as to the extent of the damage. By the time Killian made his way back to Stacey, the doctor had been in, and a nurse was cleaning Stacey's wound. Thankfully it was a new gash, not the other one, since it would be problematic to restitch a wound that old. But a new one with fresh margins could get new stitches, and, as long as she took it easy, both would heal.

He sighed as he stared at her. "You know you'll have to stay here," he said.

She looked at him, frowned, and said, "In your dreams."

He grinned. "Feisty, I like that."

"Well, it sure as hell isn't a cabin in the middle of nowhere," she said.

"*Hmm*, we're not up for that yet either," he said. "We need to nab James Dean first."

"I think he'll disappear into the woodwork," she announced.

"You think so?" He pondered that and said, "The trouble is, we won't know."

"Well, I still need to get away and heal for a bit. Is there any reason we can't go away for a few days anyway?"

"What about your father?"

At that, she immediately gasped and said, "You're right. I can't go anywhere."

"At least not until we know how he's doing," he said gently.

She nodded slowly. "What's wrong with me?" she asked. "We just brought him in, and I'm already trying to get away."

"No," he said. "Listen. You're just looking to get out of this high-stress scenario. To get away from all the torment and the craziness to find a bit of peace and quiet. Don't confuse that with anything else. You're not trying to get away from your father. You're trying to survive. You desperately need a respite from all the madness."

She nodded slowly. "You're right," she said. "I guess that makes more sense than anything. I just … How do you deal with this, when it just never quits?"

"In some ways you get used to it," he said. "And, in other ways, you never do. In my world, it's what I do. So I'm used to it."

She nodded. "It's crazy," she said. "You must be very good."

"I … like to think so," he said, flashing her a big grin.

She stared at him. "I still want to get to know you."

"That's a given," he said immediately. He reached out, and she immediately slipped her hand into his. When the nurse started deep-cleaning the wound, Stacey gripped Killian's fingers tighter, and he just let her. He gently stroked the hair from her face. "Don't dwell on it," he said. "It'll be over soon."

"Maybe," she said. "But, man, oh man, in the meantime, it hurts."

"It does," the nurse said briskly. "But I'm pretty sure you were supposed to be staying home and taking care of that wound, not out in the woods getting new ones."

"I was," she said, "but my father's life was in jeopardy."

At that, the woman's face softened, and she nodded. "The things we do for our loved ones."

"There's nobody else in the world, if I don't have him," Stacey said quietly.

Killian thought about that and realized just how true it was. "You must have felt very alone—in your marriage, I mean." By now, the nurse had finished stitching up Stacey's new wound and was now cleaning up the area once more.

Stacey sighed as the local shot of painkiller must have kicked in. She released her vice grip on Killian's hand. He patted her hand now. "Yes. So very alone," she said. "But that stage of my life is over, and you can't imagine the joy of knowing that Max is gone and that I don't have to deal with him or the fear of him ever again."

"Nope," he said. On that note, he pulled out his phone and sent off a message regarding the estate. If she wasn't divorced, then somebody needed to be looking out for her interests, before James Dean—and whoever else was in this guy's slimy circle of friends—tried to cut Stacey out of the material wealth that Max had left behind.

If any of it had been obtained legally.

If it were stolen, or related to arms dealing, it would all be seized by the government anyway. But Killian could count on the Mavericks to check into that. With that done, he pocketed his phone and looked down to see her watching him with a frown. He smiled, then leaned over and kissed her on the forehead. "Just checking a few things."

"Always working," she groused.

"That is the reality of life with me," he said seriously. "When I'm on a job, I'm on a job. When I'm off, I'm off."

"Do you have the same intensity and focus when you're off a job?"

He grinned. "Depends what I'm focusing on," he said, waggling his eyebrows in a comical manner.

She burst out laughing. "Well, in that case," she said, "you're forgiven. And, when it's just the two of us, will you turn that same intensity on me?"

"Guaranteed."

The nurse burst out laughing. "You two are funny," she said. "Been together for a while?"

"Actually, we haven't," Stacey confessed, "but we certainly hit it off."

"It's like that sometimes," the nurse said comfortably. "Just don't waste the opportunity. You've had one of those lessons in how fast life can change and how fragile it is. And remember what you said about how, without your loved ones, what is there? You remember that when it comes time to dealing with problems and other headaches in life."

"Will do," Stacey said quietly. "I've had more than a few lessons on hardships, and I'm all about finding the good things now."

"You have to work at those too," the nurse said. "But it looks like you two have a solid groundwork to make that happen." She beamed at them. "Sit tight, and I'll be back in a few minutes."

"Interesting how everybody else keeps telling us what we weren't so quick to recognize ourselves," she murmured.

Killian nodded. "Hatch has been urging me to hook up with you since day one."

"I'm not sure what *hook up* even means anymore," she said.

"All he meant was that he saw a special spark between us and that I should pursue it, after the case was done."

"And I kind of took over and got ahead of his plan then, didn't I?"

"Hey, I'm okay with that. Equal rights and all," he said. "I'm not a sexist. You want to ask me out? Then go for it."

She chuckled. "I'm pretty sure I asked you to go away with me."

"And I'm a man of opportunity, and I'll never look a gift horse in the eye, mouth, whatever it is."

She rolled her eyes at him. "You need to shut up now, before you get yourself in trouble," she said.

He burst out laughing. "See? And you don't pull your punches either."

"Of course not," she said, smiling. "I spent a lot of time in fear. I don't ever want to be afraid again."

"No fear allowed," he agreed. "You've got a problem with me? You tell me flat-out."

"And you'll never hit me, right?"

He looked at her steadily. "Sweetheart, I have never hurt a woman in my life. Even if they're the bad guy."

And it looked like she believed him, but he knew it would take more than just words to prove it. It was something she would have to learn slowly. Trusting again was a big deal, and she'd have to take her time. That was okay because he was up for seeing how they did along the way. She was special, and definitely they shared a connection between them that he didn't want to let go of.

Only time would tell what would happen where James Dean was concerned. Killian wanted Dean cleared off this case and for her to be completely out of danger. On that note he pulled out his phone again, calling Jerricho directly, putting his phone on speaker, asking if they had checked the satellite feeds yet.

"Satellite feeds checked. James Dean left when the sirens arrived."

"Good. Can the team track him, figure out where he went to?"

"They're working on that right now," he said. "We'll put a guard on Stacey's father, as he'll be staying in the hospital for a while." Then Jerricho hung up.

"And what about a guard around Hatch?" she asked curiously. "Or is he so invincible that he doesn't need a guard?"

"Hatch's coming with us," Killian said. "He's hurt, but he's not that bad."

She shook her head. "I don't want him injured anymore."

"You may not want him injured, but, if you ever imply that he can't do the job," Killian said, "you'll have a hell of a fight on your hands."

She sighed. "All this macho stuff, I'm not really used to it."

"Well, better get used to it," he said, "if you're hanging around with us." And he leaned over and kissed her.

"What the hell was that?" she said in exasperation. "That was like a little baby kiss, like I'm a ... I'm a kid with a boo-boo or something."

"Oh, and how did you want to get kissed?" he asked, lifting an eyebrow.

She gave him an impish grin. "Like we're all alone, like

we have all the time in the world, and like you really mean it."

"Well, I can give you one of those," he said. "Like I really mean it." And, with that, he gathered her up in his arms and kissed her passionately. When the nurse returned and cleared her throat loudly, he pulled back. He glanced at the nurse, who eyed the two of them enviously.

"You know that there's a time and a place, and this is not it," she said.

He looked down to see a bemused look on Stacey's face.

"Wow," she said. "I did ask for that," she murmured. "And that was a hell of a kiss."

"It was," the nurse said. "And now you make me want to go home to my husband."

"And that's what you should do," he said quietly. "Life's too short for all of this pain without more pleasure."

"When my shift's over," she said, "I'll remember that. Now that those wounds are cleaned up and dry, I've come to bandage them, the new and the old."

He looked down at Stacey and said, "I'll leave you for a few minutes, while I go check on Hatch."

"Good," she said. "Especially if he's coming with us, we've got to make sure that he'll be okay too."

He grinned. "He'd be thrilled that you care."

"No, he just wants someone to argue with," she said, laughing.

And, on that note, he kissed her forehead and headed out to check on his friend.

CHAPTER 12

"I COULD HAVE told him that Hatch is doing just fine, but he looks like the kind of guy who wants to see for himself," the nurse said to Stacey.

"That's so true," Stacey said, with a smile. As soon as her leg was bandaged again, she looked at the nurse and asked, "Is Hatch likely to be released?"

"It's more a case of we won't hold him," she said, her lips twitching. "I've seen guys like that before. They come in, get patched up, and, next thing you know, they're gone, even though any normal human being would need two days of recovery," she said, with an eye roll. "Just something about them. They're larger-than-life somehow. Stronger, smarter, faster. I don't know. It's... They're just a completely different breed. *Warriors*," the nurse added quietly. "And, when you get a chance to match up with one, like you obviously have, you hang on for the ride. It'll be wild. It'll be tumultuous, but it will be the ride of a lifetime. If you can make it last, they're excellent partners, a true gift from God."

"Are they?" she asked hopefully. "Because I'm coming out of a really ugly marriage."

"I heard some of the details," she said. "These guys focus and train, so they know exactly where to direct the anger they have, and it's not at their women," she said firmly.

"I hope you're right," she said, "because I really, really

like him."

"I'd say you're well past the *like* stage," the nurse said, with a smile. "And, if that kiss was anything to go by, you guys need some quiet time and space, where you can get rid of all that pent-up energy."

"Well, that was the hope," she said. "And now that my husband has been killed, I don't have to look over my shoulder quite so much anymore."

"Good," she said. "So it's time to get away for a few days, where you can heal that leg and explore the relationship, like you both obviously want to."

"That's the plan, but I also need to know that Hatch and my father will be okay too."

"Your father is in good hands," she said. "And, short of us finding anything more severe in the x-rays, he'll stay here with us for a few days. As long as he's under guard and there's no other danger, he should be good to go next week."

"That would make me very happy,' she said quietly. "There's just the two of us."

"And we'll do everything we can for him," she said, with a bright smile. She stepped back, cleaned up her mess, and said, "Now I think you're good to go too."

Stacey slowly slid off the hospital bed, walked a few steps, and said, "I still don't understand that phenomenon. How come I didn't feel any pain at all, until the new wound was pointed out to me? I feel like such an idiot to only feel pain when I see the injury."

"Because that's when your brain connected," the nurse explained. "Like so many things in life, you don't see it until it's pointed out to you, and then, when you do have it pointed out, it makes so much more sense."

"I guess." When the curtain opened up, she turned, and

there was Killian. "How's Hatch?"

"He's fine, and he's ready to leave with us."

"Perfect," she said. "Look. I've got pretty bandages now."

He shook his head. "It would sure be great if you could stop getting hurt on my watch."

"You're not responsible for this," she said. "That asshole cut me."

"Oh, and, by the way, that asshole's been picked up."

She stopped and stared. "The one who kidnapped me from the ferry?"

"Yep, *John Smith*. An alias obviously but one all law enforcement is using to collect more data on him and to connect his cases all over the place. He's not a very happy camper."

"And why is that?"

"Apparently he kept a logbook with him, listing who and what he was up to," he said. "So now the police have enough to charge him."

"Was he in California?"

"No, the Vancouver police picked him up. He was trying to get on another ferry."

"Jesus. Why? So he could kidnap another woman?"

"He did say something about your case, by the way. That you just fell into his lap, when he realized what was going on."

"So he just had to jump in there and take advantage of the situation? God forbid he could have actually helped me instead."

"Like I said, some people are like that."

"That's two down," she said. "If only we could get James Dean."

"Everybody's out looking for him, so it will only be a matter of time."

She looked up, then looked away.

"What is it?" he asked. "Come on. Something's bothering you. What is it?"

She nodded, then took a deep breath. "Honestly I feel like the only way we'll find him is when he comes after me."

"We don't know that he's coming after any of us. Now that Max is dead, his life will get torn apart, including any connections between the two of them. The best thing James could do is to leave the country."

"Do you really think he would do that?" she asked hopefully. Because, in her mind, if he just left and never came back, that would be perfect. She definitely didn't want to be looking over her shoulder for the rest of her life. And, as she'd already told Killian, something was really scary about James Dean. Max was scary, but James Dean was terrifying. Maybe because she had witnessed Dean killing an armed man with his hands. "We can leave now then?"

"Yep, that's what we're doing. But you can't say goodbye to your father."

She winced at that. "Why not?"

"He's getting scans done right now."

She sagged in place. "Can we come back tonight?"

"We'll be at a safe house for now," he said. "With any luck, you can talk to him on the phone tonight."

She had to be happy with that. Moving slowly, they headed out the front exit, where they found Hatch sitting on the bench there.

He looked up, a little wan, a little tired, and grinned at her. "See? I'm here."

"You shouldn't be," she scolded.

"Neither should you," he said, motioning at her leg.

She winced at that. "I'll heal better at home," she muttered.

"Yeah, you and me both," he said.

She rolled her eyes. Killian laughed and said, "Both of you, sit here for a minute, and I'll bring the vehicle around." He was gone all of two minutes, and, by the time he got back, the two of them were wrangling again.

As they got in the vehicle, Hatch said, "At least she has a temper."

"Oh, does that make me somebody you approve of then?"

"I approved of you from the beginning," he said. "It's just been a matter of getting you guys to see it."

"We see it already," she said, "so why are you still hassling us?"

"I would hardly call it hassling you," he said. "I just want to make sure that you are really who you say you are."

She stopped, looked at him, and asked, "What do you mean?"

"Killian's been hurt before," Hatch said quietly. "And I want to make sure that you're here for the right reasons."

"I am definitely here for the right reasons," she said. "He fascinates me."

"Maybe, but what happens when that wears off?"

"Well, I'd like to think it wouldn't," she said. "He is the exact opposite of what I married before, so that should tell me something."

"It does," he said. "But Killian's a good man, and he has a big heart. I don't want to see you smash it."

"No," she said, as she opened up the passenger door. "I don't either."

"So, when somebody hands you their heart," Hatch said, "you have a duty to look after it."

She smiled. "Ditto, in reverse."

"Are you guys getting in?" Killian asked in exasperation.

She looked up at him and smiled, then said, "No, we're having a conversation. Do you mind?"

He stared at her in shock for a moment, then burst out laughing.

But Hatch hopped in the back seat, and she climbed into the front, both of them wincing, grimacing from the pain.

"Good Lord," Killian said. "The two of you are quite the pair."

"We're fine," both Hatch and Stacey snapped in perfect unison, slamming their doors shut.

Killian looked from one to the other, grinned, and said, "Well, this ought to be fun. Two invalids and neither one of you will be good about it."

"As if you'd be any different," Hatch scoffed.

"Hell no, I wouldn't," he said, "but I'm not the one who ran into a bullet this time."

"Lucky shot," Hatch said.

Such good-natured teasing was in his voice that she had to wonder at these men who dealt with this kind of thing all the time. Because they were calm and relaxed about it, it was easier on her too. "Well, I didn't get shot," she said. "So you can't blame it on me."

"No, but you went and injured that leg again," Hatch said, with a shake of his head. "What's up with that?"

"Fine," she said. "We're all idiots then."

"Well, I don't think there's any argument about that," Killian said.

As they drove downtown and away from the hospital, she asked, "Where are we going?"

"A safe house."

"Well, you said that before, and, as descriptions go, that really isn't helpful."

"You'll see when we get there," he said.

"I'm not allowed to know the address?"

"Nope, you never know when or where bugs have been planted."

At that, she stopped and stared at him. She sat back in her seat in complete silence. Finally, when they came to a stop, they were in the underground parking lot of a large apartment complex. They parked very close to an elevator. As they slowly made their way out, Killian came around to help her and Hatch. They managed to get inside the elevator and headed up without seeing anybody. As they got to the top, he held a finger to his lips, and she watched as he opened the double doors that led to a penthouse directly inside. She frowned at that. And he turned, locked the doors behind them, and then brought something from his pocket, completely searching the small space. Finally he came back and said, "It's clear."

"Good thing," Hatch said, "because I'm really not in the mood to run."

"Neither am I," she said. "Are you guys always this thorough?"

"We have to be," Killian said. "Being vigilant keeps us alive."

She nodded. "Got it. I need to stay alive too, and that means getting my ass on that couch over there," she said, as she hobbled forward. When she finally sank down in place, she sighed happily.

"And that's why you should have stayed in the hospital and rested," Killian murmured.

"Nope, not happening. But I do have pain pills, and I didn't get those yet."

He immediately went and got her a glass of water and handed over two of the pills.

"I have antibiotics too, I think," she murmured.

"Yeah, you do, and I'll get those in a minute," he said. "They're in the other bags."

Then he turned, and, as she watched, Killian doled out medication for Hatch. "Look at that," she said. "You fill the role of nursemaid very well."

He glared at her. "I do it because I have to," he said, "but don't get any ideas."

She chuckled. "Hey, I sure don't plan on getting hurt anymore."

"Ha," he said, "if you don't listen to instructions, you will."

"Maybe," she said, shifting on the couch pillows. "You don't mind if I sleep right now, do you?"

"No," he said. "Not at all." As he walked to her, he smiled, then leaned over and gave her gentle kiss on the forehead and said, "Sweet dreams."

⚓

KILLIAN TURNED, FINDING Hatch grinning at him. Killian shrugged. "I don't know how it happened," he said, "but it did."

"And it's a good thing," Hatch said. "I really like her."

"Too bad. She's taken."

At that, Hatch burst out laughing. "She's also had a pretty good idea with that nap thing."

"You want to move into one of the bedrooms, or will you crash on the other couch?"

He looked at it and said, "I'll sleep better in the bed." Then he headed for the nearest bedroom.

At that, Killian found himself alone at the kitchen table. Within what seemed like a few minutes, though it was likely longer, his phone buzzed with an incoming message from Jerricho. Killian swore softly as he read it. He wouldn't wake anybody with the news, but it was concerning. He quickly typed back a question. **How badly hurt is the guard?**

And got a response right away. **He'll live. So will the father; he was unconscious at the time. Since the attempt was unsuccessful, we'll really have to keep an eye out, assuming he'll try again.**

Interesting that Dean went after the father again, Killian wrote.

He probably knows how much Stacey loves him. So it's all about her, causing her pain, getting back at her for blowing up the life Dean was living.

Killian nodded, rubbing his face before replying. **Any results from Max's house?**

Just a lot of questions, nothing really sure yet. Forensics is all over it.

Great, he replied, frowning. **That could take quite a while.**

It could, and, if Hatch was okay, I'd send you both to take a look into the house yourselves.

Give him a couple hours. He's grabbing a nap right now.

How badly hurt is he?

More pissed that he was caught by a bullet.

Of course, Jerricho said. **We'll keep an eye on the**

progress at Max's, and we'll find you a pathway there.

And a guard here.

Or else you go alone and leave Hatch with her? Jerricho suggested.

That might be the best answer, but let's give Hatch a few hours. Even then, Killian turned at a sound to see Hatch coming out of the bedroom.

"What's new?" he asked.

Killian quickly filled him in.

"You might as well go now," Hatch said. "I tried to sleep, but it didn't work. I'll put on some coffee. You better get back before she wakes up."

Rolling his eyes at that, Killian sent a message off to Jerricho. **Heading out now. Hatch's up already.**

Killian was already dressed in his fatigues and was down the elevator, into the garage, and out of the building in a matter of seconds. He took an alternate route out this time. As he headed to Max's home, he recalled the layout he had studied, though he'd never been there before. He used GPS to navigate to the address, and, by the time he pulled up one block away, he left the vehicle, carrying just a small backpack of essentials. He walked down the alleyway, looking to see if anybody else was around.

According to the team updating him through a headset, the house was empty.

"What about the cops and forensics and all?"

"They were there but left already. They'll probably be back tomorrow."

"Right. It's not like there's any rush. The owner's dead. Was anybody else in the house?"

"According to them, no."

"Animals?"

"No way because, outside of some big-ass dogs or something, nothing else would go with Max's image."

As Killian walked through the backyard, he kept to the shadows, just in case anybody watched the property. Getting inside the house was incredibly easy, but then the cops had turned off the security system and hadn't reset it. Killian walked through the ground floor, but he was looking for the office, looking for that secret space where Max would have kept anything of importance.

He didn't find it on the first go-round, but the house was a split-level design, with multiple levels staggered throughout, with small staircases in different places. As he quickly explored the extended spaces, he checked through the master bedroom suite but found no safe, nothing in the night table. As a matter of fact, it was oddly clean. The guy had been fastidious about neatness apparently.

Killian moved down a level, and there, in the office, he stopped because the cops had been through here but had left it relatively unscathed. If it had been him, he would have torn the plaster off the walls, looking for anything that this guy might have left hidden. He was a slimy bastard, but then the cops probably didn't know that.

As Killian walked through the office, he tapped the walls and finally came to a spot which sounded ever-so-slightly on the hollow side. He checked the edge of the paneling and very quickly found a hidden mechanism that popped it open. Once it did, he whistled because, in front of him, was a safe and several cupboards. He opened up the cupboards first. One was full of ledgers and other bookkeeping materials. The second one held a series of small black books, all empty. And then he came to the safe, and it didn't take him too long to crack it. He swung open the door to reveal it was full of cash but nothing else. He once more whistled at that. After taking photos of everything, he closed the safe and locked it up again. Then he checked out the ledgers. The first one was all about arms dealing.

He sent photographs to Jerricho. **Lots of evidence here.**

Anything that points to where Dean would be?
Not in this. I'm headed to the desk next.

With the cupboards closed, he shut the hidden door, and he quickly moved to the huge desk. Knowing that Dean was a friend to Max, somebody who he knew really well, what would he even have written down here on his friend? What Killian and his team really needed was an address, a location, but that's not something most criminals would write down. An old Rolodex was here, which Killian thought was interesting, suggesting that perhaps Max didn't quite trust computers.

Killian flipped through the Rolodex, looking for Dean's name, or any other names close to it, but didn't see anything. Pulling open the right-hand drawer to the desk, he found just office supplies, and the big long drawer at his waist held loose papers and pads. In the bottom drawer was a series of files. He flipped through the folders, stopping when a name caught his eye.

Dean.

Killian popped out the folder and looked through it, taking photos while speed-reading it. Had the cops even looked at this? Or were they planning on coming back with somebody else on another day? Killian didn't understand. Maybe they hadn't even seen the Dean label. It was partially buried under another sticker.

Killian went through the contents of this folder, which

included information on business dealings between Max and his buddy Dean. And, boy, were they in deep into a lot of different companies. But right there was Dean's social security number and banking information. Killian quickly took photos of all that, still looking for an address or a cell phone number.

But he found nothing.

Scrawled across the very back page, it said, *new cell phone* and listed a number.

Quickly he forwarded the number to Jerricho with a message. **Trace this. See if you can get a tracker on it.** He kept going through the files, taking photos, and, when his phone rang with a call from Jerricho, he answered it.

"Get out *now*."

Killian didn't even think twice about it or ask a single question. He simply bolted through the office window that led to the backyard. He had reached the side gate when a series of gunfire crashed through the air, shattering the office windows.

He ducked over the fence and headed down to his vehicle, the phone to his ear. "What the hell did you find?"

"We tracked that phone number you sent. It was outside the house, when I called you," he said. "And now it's inside the house."

"Shit," he said. "In that case, I want to go back in again."

"Watch your back."

He turned and headed back toward the house.

He checked the office first, to see if Dean was there, because obviously he wanted to pull information from his buddy's house. As Killian swept through the bottom of the house, he didn't see anything. But the file that he had left on the desk was gone. He raced around to the front of the house, just as a vehicle pulled away from the curb. He stopped long enough to check the make and model, and then holding the phone to his ear, he passed the details on the vehicle to Jerricho, as Killian ran back to his vehicle. "Trace it," he said. "I'm just getting into mine now. He grabbed the file that I had open on the desk, when I bailed."

"Did you get any photos?"

"All of it," he said. "only on the last page did I find that phone number. I'll send those photos as soon as I get a minute."

"Good," he said. "If he's smart, Dean will be running for another country. But, if he's greedy, he might not be ready to give up everything he's got going here."

"A ton of cash is in the safe. And I found a lot of bank accounts and lots of dealings involved. The real question is whether or not Max had a will."

"Why?"

"Because Stacey and Max were not divorced," he said. "The bastard wouldn't sign any papers."

"Good," Jerricho said. "We'll make sure that we get her as much as we can."

"*If* there's anything left after the authorities are done with it," he murmured.

"Yeah, they've always got to get their cut of the pie first. But only if it's criminal and only if they can prove it belongs to anybody else."

"Stay with me while I put the phone in the holder." Killian drove, following his instincts as to where Dean may have gone. When he came out onto the main road, he swore and said, "No sign of him."

"We haven't picked him up on satellite yet either."

"Shit," he said.

"Wait, hang on." At that, Jerricho added, "Go forward two blocks and pull off to the right."

Killian went forward two blocks to a large space up ahead. "What am I looking for?"

"The vehicle is parked about six cars ahead of you."

"Shit," he said. "In that case, he's probably gone." But he got out and slowly approached the vehicle, and, sure enough, it was empty. He kicked the tires in outrage.

"Now," Jerricho said. "Get back and look after Hatch and Stacey. We'll send a team into Max's house, to ensure we get as much information as we can. The cops come second on this now," he said. "We've got international arms deals, according to some of the information you sent."

"Good," Killian said. "Secure that house. It's still Stacey's primary residence at this point, now that Max's gone."

"We're on it."

And, with that, angry that he had missed Dean, Killian drove back to the safe house. He pulled into the underground lot, then used a different elevator system which would require two elevators to get up there. By the time he got back to the penthouse, he was frustrated and edgy. He walked in to see Hatch sitting at the kitchen table, sipping coffee.

Hatch looked at him and said, "Uh-oh. How bad?"

"Bad enough," Killian said. "But I got lots of information and sent off a ton of photographs to Jerricho, only to finally find a phone number. They traced it right to the same damn property, where Dean was probably watching me the whole time."

Hatch whistled. "Jesus. I presume he didn't have a clear

shot at any time, since he didn't take it."

"No, but he shot into the house, seconds after Jerricho called me to get out."

"Maybe temper."

"More to chase me away, I think. But once I realized he'd gotten into the house, I knew he was probably looking for something, so I went right back in but missed him. I'm pissed at myself for that too. When they called and said to get the hell out, I just bolted, which gave James the opening. Anyway, we had his vehicle ID'd, but he got away." Pacing around, Killian filled in his partner on the rest of it, as Hatch sat there. "A ton of cash is in the safe, plus tons of paperwork on arms-dealing information and other businesses that he's been running with his buddy."

"That's what James was after then," Hatch said.

"Yep, but, at least," Killian said, with a grin, "I'd already gotten copies of it on my phone, and I've sent it all off to Jerricho."

"That's huge," he said. "So not a bad outing."

"No, not necessarily. But, at the same time, I missed him. Again."

"It's okay," he said. "He's after stuff, and he's making mistakes. We'll get him."

"I hope so." Killian looked over at Stacey, still on the couch. "How's she doing?"

"She hasn't stirred at all."

"She doesn't look very comfortable there. I feel like I should get her into bed."

"Go for it," he said. "I wouldn't mind a lie down myself, if you're up for standing watch for a while."

"Yep, just let me get her moved to the bed." And, with that, he bent down and scooped her up. When she murmured, he whispered, "It's okay. Just go to sleep." And she nodded off again.

"For somebody who's been through what she has," Hatch said, "she's pretty trusting."

"That's how she got into such trouble in the first place," Killian said. "But at least now she's trusting the right people."

He carried her into the second bedroom and laid her on the bed. Taking a blanket folded at the foot of the bed, he covered her up, then gave her a gentle kiss on the forehead.

CHAPTER 13

STACEY WOKE UP in pain, heat searing up and down her leg. She lay here, gasping for a few minutes, trying to figure out where she was. She threw off the blanket, since even the weight of it on her leg was killing her. She took several long slow breaths, trying to regain control, as she studied the room around her, confused and disoriented. She couldn't even begin to figure out where she was. She slowly sat up, grateful that she wasn't tied up, as the fear and the trauma of her kidnappings surfaced again.

She wanted desperately to cry out, but that could bring the attention of somebody she didn't want.

Slowly she stood and made her way to the en suite bathroom. She looked at her face in the mirror, shuddered, then used the facilities and washed up. When she stepped back into the bedroom, she let out a squeak.

Instantly Killian raced across the room. "Hey, it's okay. It's me," he said.

She collapsed in his arms and cried. After a few moments, she got control again. "I woke up," she said, "hurting so bad, and in a strange room. I didn't know where I was, or who I was with, so I immediately thought the worst." She shook her head. "When will this ever end?"

"Soon," he said. "Come on. Let's get you back to bed."

She sighed and let him lead her to bed. "I'll go get your

medicine again," he said, and he quickly disappeared. She sat up against the headboard, more shaken than she wanted to admit. The trauma of her kidnapping seemed destined to torment her nights now too. And her days, if she were honest. When he returned, he held out the pills and a glass of water. She quickly popped them back and then crashed on the pillows. "I'm not even sure I'm sleepy anymore," she said. "That woke me up, like wide awake."

"Understood," he said.

"What are you doing still up?"

"I had four hours' sleep, and I just switched with Hatch. He's fine, by the way," he said, before she asked. "And it's morning as well."

She looked at him in surprise.

Then he walked over and opened up the blinds.

It was clearly daylight outside. "Oh," she said, feeling foolish. "And here I thought it was still the middle of the night."

"Nope, we're all good."

"If you say so," she said.

"How about some coffee then?"

With that, she tried to sit back up.

Immediately he forestalled her efforts and said, "Hey, I'm playing nursemaid today, remember? I'll go put on some fresh coffee, and I'll bring you a cup in a minute."

"Fine," she muttered. And she was honestly grateful. With her leg still as painful as it was, she could use the rest. Although, she had to admit, the original injury itself was feeling a bit better today. It looked kind of nasty, but the pain for the worst cut was definitely easing back. It was the combination of the new one that hurt so bad today. Yet she sighed happily, as she rolled over and just stretched out. It was good to be safe. Even with the residual stress she had from waking up so badly, now that she knew she was okay, she was starting to relax. When she heard a crash in the kitchen, she called out, "Killian, is that you?"

"Yeah, it's me," he said. "Sorry, I just dropped a cup."

She sighed. "You keep doing that," she said, "and I'll never recover."

He came back and said, "Here is the last cup from the pot already on, and I started a fresh one." Then he added, "Here. Let me help you sit up a little. Come here. You'll be fine. Just relax."

"I know. I know," she said, but it was hard to uncoil the tension inside her. "Any news?"

"More than news," he said. And he sat down with his cup of coffee and perched on the edge of the bed and told her all that had occurred while she'd been sleeping.

She stared at him in shock. "And Dean got away again," she wailed.

"I know," he said grimly. "Believe me. I know."

She immediately reached out a hand and said, "It's not your fault."

"Well, Jerricho said *get out,* so I wasn't sure what was happening, whether the house was being blown up or what," he said. "But I went back after Dean, when I figured out what was truly going on. Then I followed him and found his vehicle, but he had already disappeared from there. So I don't know if he got into another vehicle or not. He's wily. He's been doing this for a long time," he said.

"You think so?" she asked.

"Yep, I'm just thinking about the Interpol rap sheet. I can't even remember all his history."

"Well, I know he was really, really close with Max. It's

like they were blood brothers or something."

"Exactly. They were bound by a passion for hurting people, something that most people can't admit. And, when somebody like that finds another soul mate, they tend to bond, very, very tightly."

"Well, that was them."

"But your husband is dead," he said gently. "I've spoken to the hospital, and your father is doing just fine. He's stronger this morning but definitely needs a few days to rest. He's got a couple broken ribs, a broken wrist, and he took a bit of a beating last night. A few welts, a few bumps, but he will be okay."

She stared at him, as tears crept into her eyes. Oh thank heavens. She couldn't find it in her heart to feel anything but relief over her husband. But her father… and a beating at the hospital? At least he was safe now. "My God," she said. "I'm so grateful. Can I see him?"

"Just give him time to heal now," he said. "Maybe later, when this is over, not today," he quickly corrected himself. "But, in a couple days, we can go to the hospital, so you can visit."

"You think I can talk to him on your phone?"

"Probably," he said. "This is the new one that I picked up." He considered it for a moment and then said, "Better not. We need to keep this clear for high-priority calls," he said. "It's the one that I was called on to get out of Max's house. I just don't want anything to track it. We can get you a disposable phone."

"I guess," she said.

"You can use mine to play games or something, if you want to just sit here and rest."

"No," she said. "Well, can I use it for—" Then she

stopped and handed it back and said, "No, I don't want to do anything that might get us noticed."

"It's probably not a case of this phone being tracked," he said, with a shrug.

"No, it's okay," she said. "Whenever you get another phone maybe. Will it be today?" she asked hopefully.

"I've already asked for two new burner phones."

"Why don't you make that three?" she said, with a sigh.

"Well, I have an encrypted laptop you can log on to check your emails and stuff, if you want."

"That would be good."

He got up, walked out to the living room, picked up a laptop for her, and came back.

"It's amazing just how hard it is to be disconnected from the world," she murmured.

"It is, indeed."

And feeling a little bit like the previous days after she'd been held captive, she spent the day recovering, just resting. By the time nighttime rolled around again, she said, "I feel incredibly lazy. I don't know of a time in my life that I've ever spent this much time in bed."

"Well," he said, "obviously you need the rest."

"I do." Later on that night, when he came in with her pain pills, she smiled and said, "You sure make a great nursemaid."

"Thank you," he said, with a gentle smile.

She shook her head. "No, I mean it. You're a very compassionate man."

He raised an eyebrow but didn't say anything, just gave her a little shrug that basically said he didn't know what she was talking about.

She laughed. "And I am feeling much better."

"Well, you've slept, eaten, and slept some more today," he said. "You should start to feel better."

"It doesn't look very pretty though."

"Your legs are gorgeous," he said. "Absolutely nothing any stitches will do to mar them."

"Says you," she scoffed. "Look at that? Anytime I wear shorts, it'll be a huge, thick, ugly line."

"Nope, it'll fade down to a thin line before you know it," he said. "I wouldn't worry about it. Besides, it's a small price to pay for being alive. Ask Hatch if he'd rather not have those scars or be alive. On second thought, don't. You might get more than you bargained for. He's been through a lot to look as good as he does."

"That kind of puts it all in perspective, doesn't it?" she said, with a nod. She laid back down again and said, "You know what? I'm not even tired."

"That's what you said this afternoon, when you crashed too."

"True. Well, I'll try to sleep, but, if I can't, I'll get up."

"You do that," he said. "We'll be in the living room, working."

"Fine, I don't really know what work you can do though."

"We're helping track all the cases from the John Smith guy, who kidnapped you off the ferry."

"Good," she said. "Make sure you nail his ass to the wall."

"Well, there is some talk that he was supposed to come back down here."

"Why is that?"

"Apparently, according to the authorities, your husband wasn't happy that Smith let you escape. After all, John Smith was supposed to kill you."

"If he hadn't been so greedy, taking time to get the money from my father as well, he might have done it too. He was clearly terrified of Max, and rightly so. I'm sure Max was livid when he found out. I'm surprised he didn't go after the Smith guy himself."

"Well, Max may have had something to do with the way Smith got caught."

"That would be the type of justice Max would appreciate," she said, with a nod.

"Apparently the authorities traced Smith by his burner phone, and, so far, nobody's talking about how they found his number."

"Ha," she said, with a laugh. "That would be Max for sure. And, if my kidnapper knows that, then he would probably turn around and spill his guts, if he thought there would be some paybacks—assuming he doesn't already know that Max is dead."

"That's the trick they're working on now. In the meantime, we're working on finding any other John Smith cases."

"Okay," she said.

He leaned over, gave her gentle kiss, and walked out.

She wanted a better kiss than that, but, if she would just crash and sleep again, she didn't want another night of passing out on him. But woke several hours later. When he came back in, after hearing her moving around, she looked up and said, "I'm sorry. I keep trying to go to sleep, but I'm too wired."

"Well, just try to stay quiet," he said. "Hatch is resting."

"Resting? Is that a euphemism for sleeping?"

"In this case it is because he still has to heal too."

"Right," she said. "Well, why don't you sit here and visit?" And she shifted over on the bed.

"Dangerous," he said.

"Hardly. I'm still injured."

"Not that injured," he said.

She looked at him with interest. "Really?"

He looked at her in surprise. "It wouldn't be that big of a deal," he said.

"Are you telling me that we could make love with this leg, and you wouldn't hurt me?" she asked curiously.

He laughed. "Are you asking out of curiosity or because you're interested in trying it out?"

"Oh, I'm definitely interested in trying it out," she said, a twinkle in her eye. "Particularly if Hatch's asleep."

"Well, he is. I just checked on him," he said. "But I hardly think our first time together needs to be decided based on whether a friend is sleeping or not."

"Oh, you've got a point there," she said. "Now I know you're smart, and you're really capable. So … if you think you've got this figured out?"

"Absolutely I've got this figured out," he said. And, with a surprise move, he flicked off the bedcovers, and there she was, just in her panties and a T-shirt. "Wow, that takes care of half the battle. You're already mostly undressed."

"Not quite," she said, stifling her laughter. She looped her arms around his neck, tugged him down, and said, "Remember your promise."

"Oh, I remember," he said. "And I never break a promise." And he lowered his head for a kiss. When he lifted it a few minutes later, she felt the same dizzy, all-encompassing disorientation she had felt the first time he had kissed her.

"Man," she said. "Your kisses just knock everything out of me, and I can't even think straight."

"Good," he said, and he lowered his head again.

She moaned in his arms, twisting, as she felt part of herself come alive, after months and months of fear, torment, and disbelief in her own choices. Back then she had shut everything down and wouldn't let her body respond to even the slightest attraction because it was just so hard to trust herself and those around her. She slid her arms up around Killian's neck, tugging him even closer, pressing her breasts flat against him, his arms wrapped around her, holding her close.

In a distant part of her mind, she knew the pain was likely to strike at any moment, but, so far, there hadn't been any. She pulled her head back, giving him access to her neck, as he rained kisses down her throat and on her collarbone and down to the T-shirt's edge, where he smoothly pulled it up over her shoulders and off.

Then he lowered his head yet again, noting she was in the middle of the bed, her injured leg off to the side, and he was sideways on the bed, facing her. She had no clue how he would do this, but, as long as it didn't hurt, she was happy to stay quiet and see. She didn't want to stiffen up over any of it, but, at the same time, just that little part of her mind refused to disengage, battling with another part that needed him so badly.

"Relax," he said, sliding a hand down her thigh, the injured one, and yet she could barely feel it. It was like a feather drifting across her stitched-up skin. She watched in amazement as he curled down to her calf, slid down to the bottom of her foot and then up.

"You're so gentle," she whispered.

"You're injured," he murmured right back. "An injured bird. One that needs a little bit of love and care. So just relax."

She nodded slowly and reached down to curl her fingers in his hair and tug him toward her. But instead of going to her lips, like she so desperately wanted, he kissed the tip of her left breast and latched on to her nipple. She arched up with a cry, as he suckled hard and deep. She shuddered in his arms, already feeling explosions rising up, threatening to cascade over her. She twisted in his arms. "Dear God," she whispered, holding him close.

He moved to the other breast and the same thing happened.

She murmured, "Why is it like this?"

"Because, when it's good," he said, "it's meant to be really good."

She shuddered and moaned and murmured, "I need you—now."

"No, you don't," he said. "Not yet." And he proceeded to explore her ribs, her belly button, her hips. When he slid down to the plump lips at the center of her and had a long slow taste, she shuddered, her body exploding all around her. He slid a finger inside and gently stroked her passage.

She pressed her thighs wide and whispered, "Please, please." Her hands were in his curls, as she again tried to pull him toward her. He shifted around the bed, until he stood at the end. She laughed at the sudden movement, and then, when he tucked pillows underneath her hips, so that she was at the right height, she gasped as she understood.

And he plunged in deep.

She cried out, one leg wrapped around him, the other one off to the side. She wanted him so damn desperately. And yet her body was already surfeit with emotions. As soon as he slightly withdrew and then pounded in again and repeated the motion several times, she felt a second orgasm building within her. She twisted, trying to reach for him but couldn't, as he leaned over her on the bed, careful to make sure that he didn't touch her injured leg, as he drove in higher and higher and higher. When he finally rested, on the cliff, she twisted beneath him. "Come with me," she heard.

"You too," she said. "I don't want to do it alone."

He leaned over, took her lips with his, and sent them both flying.

⚓

KILLIAN CERTAINLY HADN'T expected that to happen right now. But no way in hell he would regret it. He held her close. He felt her tears against his chest. He immediately pulled back and looked at her in shock. "Did I hurt you?"

She shook her head. "No," she said. "You were amazingly gentle and, at the same time, so passionate."

"You know I would do anything not to hurt you, right?"

"I know," she said. "At least I do now." She leaned up, kissed him gently, and said, "Thank you for making it so good."

"It's not hard to make it good," he murmured. "It's a matter of coming from the right place in your heart."

"Well, maybe that was what was wrong with my husband then," she said.

"He's gone," he said, pressing a finger to her lips. "*Shhh*, no need to think about him anymore."

She nodded and smiled. "I think I can sleep now," she murmured.

"Yeah, I imagine so," he said. "Lovemaking is usually a great sleep inducer."

She smiled and said, "What about you?"

"Nope, I'm on watch," he said. "So I'll stay here for a few minutes, but then I've got to get up."

"And it's almost morning, right?"

"It is, so I would look at getting us some breakfast."

"Do we have to order it in?"

"We'll order something in," he said. "You just rest."

"Okay." She yawned and said, "Just give me a few minutes."

"No problem."

He got up and wandered through the small apartment, checking on Hatch, who was still sleeping. Killian ordered breakfast, but this time he ordered it through the Mavericks, knowing that somebody needed to take a look and make sure that everything was okay before they started taking deliveries. As he waited for that to come, he sat down with their to-do list.

One of the loose threads that they still had to sort out was the guy Killian had put the tracker on. It really bugged him because something was just so bizarre about him. As he sat here thinking about it, an idea crossed his mind. Of course. It was so far-fetched it didn't make any sense, and, because it didn't make any sense, he felt he needed to look closer at it because, dammit, nothing here made sense.

They didn't have any answers as to where Dean came into all this. Sure, Max was his buddy and all that, but still—

Just then came a knock on the door.

Hatch came out of the bathroom, looked at him, and said, "I presume that's breakfast?"

"Yeah," he said. "It is."

Killian got up, walked to get plates and to put them on the table, and, when he turned to the door, Hatch stood in the doorway looking at him, a gun against his head.

"Wow," Hatch said. "Security is not like it used to be."

Behind Hatch, holding the gun, was none other than Dean.

He pushed Hatch inside, toward where Killian was.

Killian looked at him and said, "Well, there you are." He stopped and stared and said, "Turn your head to the side."

"Fuck you," Dean said, but he did turn his head ever-so-slightly.

"Now I get it." Then he shook his head. "No. I mean, I get it, but I don't get it."

"Of course you don't get it," he said. "You're too damn stupid to get anything."

"Well, I don't know about that," he said. "But maybe you should tell me why you were following her kidnapper."

At that, Hatch looked at Killian. "What?"

"This is the guy I put the tracker on," he said. "I didn't quite see it within the shadows of the park, but, just now, with that angle, that's him."

"You are too damn smart for your own good," Dean said, with a sneer.

"What the hell?" Hatch said, looking from Dean to Killian.

"Come on. Tell me why," Killian said.

"Because when the second kidnapper made contact," Dean said, "we needed to see exactly what he was up to."

"And you wanted proof that he'd killed Stacey, I suppose."

"Well, it was the only way to put an end to this of course. Not that Max had a problem with her being dead, but he wanted to do the job himself."

"Of course. I mean, that is what he did with his first

wife, wasn't it?"

Dean glared at Killian. "You don't know anything."

"We've already pinpointed where you two buried her. It's just a matter of time before her body is dug up. You guys just love to hurt women. That bonded you together—making money illegally and hurting women, feeding power trips as the small men you are."

Dean just gave him a flick of his hand and said, "You're nothing. So where the hell is the bitch anyway?"

"I still don't understand why you didn't step in and take care of things at the exchange. You could have killed the kidnapper at the same time."

"I could have, but you were an unknown element that I didn't understand at the time. We didn't know this guy was double-crossing us and blackmailing someone else for ransom. That didn't make any sense, when we saw you arrive, so we didn't want to take out anybody until we understood just what the implications were. She is a minor cog in our wheel. But now Max is dead," he said. "And, for that, I'll make sure I take you two out as well," he snapped, taking a step forward. "Because no way in hell should Max be dead. He had forty or fifty more years left in him."

"Maybe so, but, when you live the lifestyle you do," Hatch said, "well, it's not all that unexpected."

"You didn't have to kill him," he snarled. "You didn't even know him."

"No, we didn't, but he's the kind of guy we know all too well," Killian said. "The ones who abuse women, who beat them up, and who use them as punching bags, all because they needed an outlet for their anger that day."

"She was nothing," Dean said. "No more than any of the other women he'd ever met. She was nothing to Max. The two of us were close. I knew exactly what he needed and what he was like. You know nothing."

"You loved him too, didn't you?"

"Not like that," he said in disgust. "The friendship between us nobody could understand but us. Including you guys."

"You're quite right there," he said. "But he's dead now, so that relationship is over."

"Not so much," he said, with a smirk. "It's not like you'll do anything about this right now." And Dean lifted his gun and went to pull the trigger.

As Killian caught motion out of the corner of his eye, he started to move. Hatch dropped to the ground as the gun fired, but something came out of nowhere and slammed Dean hard in the shoulder and knocked him against the wall. Killian was already on the move and quickly grasped the wrist of Dean's gun arm and slammed it hard against his knee, forcing the gun out of his hand. Then Killian immediately kicked him in the nuts and finally dropped him with a hard right clip to the jaw.

As Dean fell to the floor, Killian looked over at Stacey, standing there, the base of a shattered lamp in her hand.

She stared down at him. "I didn't kill him, did I?"

"No," he said. "You didn't."

She took a long slow deep breath. "Too damn bad," she said. "Because I really would like that to happen." She kicked him hard with her good leg. "Asshole," she muttered.

Killian laughed, picked her up in his arms, and swung her around. "It's okay. He's down, and we've got him."

Hatch walked over, checked his pulse, and said, "He's alive."

"Yeah, I just knocked him out."

Hatch rolled him over and quickly tied him up, then made some phone calls.

She sat down in a nearby kitchen chair and asked, "Does that mean we don't get food?"

Hatch looked at her and nodded. "Sorry, sweetheart. That's exactly what it means."

She glared down at the gunman. "Asshole, I'm hungry."

"Food is coming," Killian added, "but we also have a body to get rid of and people who will want to know what happened."

"That's your department," she said. "You said I can order anything I want. Well, I'm ordering peace and quiet and time away from this nightmare. So you give them all the explanations and don't involve me. I've had enough to deal with. As a matter of fact, I'll go back to bed. Let me know when breakfast is here." And, with that, she turned and walked away.

Killian looked back at Hatch, who was grinning like a fiend. "I told you that I liked her," he said. "She really knows how to rise to the occasion."

And Killian had to admit, as he looked at the gunman, that she'd done a good job. It did take a few minutes to coordinate and to get somebody involved to get Dean out of here. Killian went through Dean's pockets and pulled out the information that they needed from his wallet, including the names of lawyers. And, with that, he passed off everything to the team. When the last vehicle left, one more arrived carrying food, so he walked into the bedroom to see her lightly sleeping.

He leaned over, kissed her thoroughly, and said, "Hey, sleeping beauty, breakfast is here."

She reached out, stretched, hooked an arm around his

neck, and said, "Too bad we can't have it in bed."

Hatch cleared his throat from the bedroom doorway. "Like hell you can," he said. "I'm right here. Get your ass out of bed and come to the kitchen."

She laughed at him. "Just don't be too sour that we found each other," she warned.

"Sour? Oh hell no," he said. "I knew right from the beginning you were meant for each other, long before either of you did."

She looked up at Killian and whispered, "I did too, she said. "I just didn't trust myself anymore."

"That is no longer an issue," he said. "Nobody'll bother you again."

"I'm glad to hear that."

And he reached down and scooped her up in his arms and carried her into the kitchen.

"I'm not that badly hurt," she protested, looping her arms around his neck.

"Nope, but you shattered that lamp pretty well, and, although we cleaned it up, I don't want you to get any glass in your feet."

She chuckled. "Will you carry me around everywhere in here?"

"Well, I thought maybe we could go away for a while," he said, looking at her. "You know? Like maybe that cabin you were talking about?"

She looked at him eagerly. "When can we leave?"

"A vehicle's being prepared for us right now," he said. "But you'll need a good breakfast before we go."

She looked over at Hatch. "Are you coming too?"

"Hell no," he said, "I'm going back to my place to heal up and to commiserate on the fact that I never get the girl."

She chuckled. "You didn't want this one," she said. "We would do nothing but argue."

"You got a point there," he said, with an affectionate grin. "But it's fun arguing with you."

"Yeah," she said. "You too, and, hey, if you did want to come with us," she said magnanimously, "we'd love to have you."

At that, Killian said, "Wait, what? Who said that?"

She looked over at him and said, "I know how close you two are. So I don't have a problem with it."

"No," Hatch said gently. "Take your time, heal, rest up. I'll go do the same."

She looked at him, smiled, and said, "Your turn will come."

He shrugged. "Maybe, maybe not," he said. "I'm just happy to know that this is over and that you're safe."

She leaned a hand across, squeezed his fingers, and said, "Thank you."

He nodded, as he popped a piece of bacon into his mouth. "Now, if you won't eat, I'll steal that sausage off your plate."

"Oh no, you don't," she said, immediately picking up the wrangling that they both enjoyed. She looked over at Killian. "Are you packed?"

"Oh, yes," he said. "Packed and ready to go."

"Anywhere?" she teased.

"Anywhere you are," he said. "As long as you'll come with me, I'm happy to go on a road trip."

"Ditto," she said.

And, for her, she didn't think life could ever look better than this.

EPILOGUE

HATCH COLLAR HAD convalesced on the California base, per Mavericks' orders. He stretched out his legs and gave his arms and shoulders a good shake. It had been two weeks since the end of the last mission, and his body was back in fighting form again. And that was a damn good thing because he was raring and ready to go. Killian and Stacey had gone away for a week, and now they were back, only a couple blocks away. They were happily rearranging their lives, as they figured out what they would do.

Hatch wished them well, and what she had said—that Hatch's time would come—kept ringing in the back of his head.

The Mavericks had a bit of a running joke going on the subject. And, while nobody could do anything to force a *happily ever after* ending, Hatch really hoped that one day, maybe, if he were lucky enough, he'd find the right person for himself too.

The phone rang, and he snatched it up and saw it was Killian. "What's the matter? You bored with your time off already?" he said.

"Well, the time off was last week," he said. "Back to work now." A serious note was in his voice.

"Oh, what's up?" Hatch asked.

"An archaeologist," he said. "And his entire team."

"What about them?"

"They've disappeared out of Egypt."

"Why?"

"Well, there was talk from the government, saying that they had been arrested for doing some illegal digging and had stolen something they had found."

"Interesting, but that's hardly what I would expect an archaeologist to do."

"Exactly, but there is also talk of somebody on his team maybe having a part in it. Anyway, they were released and subsequently disappeared."

"Great. So ... what now?"

"How do you feel about Egypt?"

"I love Egypt," he said. "Am I going?"

"You are."

"And I'm looking for an archaeologist."

"And his daughter."

"Daughter?" At that his eyebrows shot up. "Okay."

"As of yesterday," Killian said, "they've been officially reported as missing."

"So who's looking for them?"

"Well, they were over there on a grant and are essentially employees of the US government. They have a very high clearance, and, now that they're missing, it's brought up some issues."

"Of course. And this isn't something they want any of the SEALs to go after or any of the other fighting teams?"

"No, they want it to be a very small, low-key investigation. In and out, quiet and fast, because they don't know whether the Egyptian government is involved somehow or not."

"Okay," he said. "That's just vague enough to keep me guessing."

"Her name is Millie, for Millicent Bragner. Her father is

Marcus Bragner."

"Oh," he said, with a whistle. "He's the one who's been a strong protester against the current Egyptian government."

"Right, which just adds to it. The US government has been trying to keep the peace, and Marcus has been causing quite a ruckus. When he was arrested, the US stepped in to try to smooth out the issues. Then he was released, and he and his daughter promptly disappeared, so now, of course, everybody's up in arms. Including the Egyptian government supposedly."

"Well, if they didn't have anything to do with it, then of course they would be. And, if they did have something to do with it, then of course they would be because they don't want anybody to know."

"Exactly," he said. "Glad you understand. By the way, you leave in three hours."

"Gee, lots of warning, huh?"

"It's the most I could get you," he said. "Even though you're going through the base."

"Military transport?"

"All the way," he said.

"Okay, I'll be there."

"I'll be your handler."

"Sounds good to me. Am I getting a partner?"

"You are," he said, with a laugh. "And somebody who hopefully will put a smile on your face."

"I'm not such a grouch that it takes much to put a smile on my face," he protested.

"Well, you haven't seen this one for quite a while."

"Do I know him?"

"Absolutely. You used to work with him."

"Says you."

"You'll meet him at the base."

"Where?"

"On the dock. You're heading out to the destroyer. And I'm not even sure which one yet. I'll text you as soon as I hear."

"How many are in shore?"

"Three."

"That's fine," he said. "Tell my partner that I'll be there."

"Wait." There was a stunned moment of silence on the other end. "You're transferring to a different base because transport's already revving up to go. We initially hadn't been given clearance. But they're giving it now."

"So how quickly am I leaving?" he asked. He looked down at his gym bag. "I only have my gym bag with me."

"No problem. Your new gear bag will be in the vehicle that picks you up."

"When is that?"

"Head out now," Killian said and hung up.

Hatch had his wallet and his phone on him, so just walked outside.

A vehicle drove up, and a head of spiky red hair and a face filled with freckles popped out.

"Jesus. Corbin?"

"Yep, that's me," he said.

"Great, are you my partner?"

"We've been partners forever anyway, so why not again?" he said. "You just haven't seen me in a bit. And I must say, they patched you up pretty well, considering."

Hatch hopped into the passenger side and said, "Yep. So, where are we going?"

"Down to the docks and out."

"It would be nice if I had enough time to get at least one change of clothes."

"In the back, mate, in the back."

He looked in the back seat and laughed. "How damn typical."

"It so is." He looked over at his buddy and said, "You ready to go kick some Egyptian ass?"

"I'm always ready to kick some ass. I don't think I've kicked any Egyptians lately."

"Well, we're only after the bad guys. So we have to keep an open mind that it's even Egyptians in this case."

"Too often in these cases people try to make the Egyptian government look bad. And they set it up so they look like the fall guy."

"I know," he said. "So what do you know about the case?"

"Only that a gorgeous chick is involved," Corbin said. "And that means I'm on board."

At that, Hatch laughed. "Well, it's my turn. If a cute chick is on board, she's mine."

"What?" Corbin said. "How come? I'm not into having to take a number here."

"Too bad," Hatch said. "I've waited a long time." He looked over at his buddy and grinned. "Besides, I'm better looking than you."

At that, the two of them burst out laughing. Even though it was a trip that would be fraught with danger and many twists and turns, Hatch was always happy to have this man watch his back. Now, if only they could get to Egypt in time and find out where the family had gone—before whoever had arranged all this decided the father and daughter were more of a liability alive than dead.

This concludes Book 15 of The Mavericks: Killian.
Read about Hatch: The Mavericks, Book 16

Hatch: Maverick (Book #16)

What happens when the very men—trained to make the hard decisions—come up against the rules and regulations that hold them back from doing what needs to be done? They either stay and work within the constraints given to them or they walk away. Only now, for a select few, they have another option:

The Mavericks. A covert black ops team that steps up and break all the rules ... but gets the job done.

Welcome to a new military romance series by *USA Today* best-selling author Dale Mayer. A series where you meet new friends and just might get to meet old ones too in this raw and compelling look at the men who keep us safe every day from the darkness where they operate—and live—in the shadows ... until someone special helps them step into the light.

Hatch is more than happy to step up and to rescue the missing father-and-daughter archeological duo. Now if only it were that easy. They'd been questioned by the Egyptian government and released, with a warning to not leave Cairo.

But, when their hotel room is found empty, most believe they took off ahead of punishment—but not Hatch's team.

When the father's foreman turns up dead, Hatch investigates the body-dump location and finds the daughter, weaving through the sand, ready to collapse.

Milly is shaken and grieving. During her captivity, her father dies, and she escapes, only to find herself lost in the sand dunes. She may be safe, but her father will never come home. Millie is determined to find the man responsible for her father's death and for the information that's changed her entire life.

Find book 16 here!
To find out more visit Dale Mayer's website.
http://smarturl.it/DMSHatch

Author's Note

Thank you for reading Killian: The Mavericks, Book 15! If you enjoyed the book, please take a moment and leave a short review.

Dear reader,

I love to hear from readers, and you can contact me at my website: www.dalemayer.com or at my Facebook author page. To be informed of new releases and special offers, sign up for my newsletter or follow me on BookBub. And if you are interested in joining Dale Mayer's Reader Group, here is the Facebook sign up page.
https://smarturl.it/DaleMayerFBGroup

Cheers,
Dale Mayer

Get THREE Free Books Now!

Have you met the SEALS of Honor?

SEALs of Honor Books 1, 2, and 3. Follow the stories of brave, badass warriors who serve their country with honor and love their women to the limits of life and death.

Read Mason, Hawk, and Dane right now for FREE.

Go here and tell me where to send them!
http://smarturl.it/EthanBofB

About the Author

Dale Mayer is a *USA Today* best-selling author, best known for her SEALs military romances, her Psychic Visions series, and her Lovely Lethal Garden cozy series. Her contemporary romances are raw and full of passion and emotion (Broken But … Mending series). Her thrillers will keep you guessing (By Death series), and her romantic comedies will keep you giggling (*It's a Dog's Life*, a stand-alone novella; and the Broken Protocols series, starring Charming Marvin, the cat).

Dale honors the stories that come to her—and some of them are crazy and break all the rules and cross multiple genres!

To go with her fiction, she also writes nonfiction in many different fields, with books available on résumé writing, companion gardening, and the US mortgage system. She has recently published her Career Essentials series. All her books are available in print and ebook format.

Connect with Dale Mayer Online

Dale's Website – www.dalemayer.com
Twitter – @DaleMayer
Facebook – facebook.com/DaleMayer.author
BookBub – bookbub.com/authors/dale-mayer

Also by Dale Mayer

Published Adult Books:

Bullard's Battle
Ryland's Reach, Book 1
Cain's Cross, Book 2
Eton's Escape, Book 3
Garret's Gambit, Book 4
Kano's Keep, Book 5
Fallon's Flaw, Book 6
Quinn's Quest, Book 7
Bullard's Beauty, Book 8
Bullard's Best, Book 9

Terkel's Team
Damon's Deal, Book 1

Kate Morgan
Simon Says… Hide, Book 1

Hathaway House
Aaron, Book 1
Brock, Book 2
Cole, Book 3
Denton, Book 4
Elliot, Book 5
Finn, Book 6
Gregory, Book 7

Heath, Book 8
Iain, Book 9
Jaden, Book 10
Keith, Book 11
Lance, Book 12
Melissa, Book 13
Nash, Book 14
Owen, Book 15
Hathaway House, Books 1–3
Hathaway House, Books 4–6
Hathaway House, Books 7–9

The K9 Files
Ethan, Book 1
Pierce, Book 2
Zane, Book 3
Blaze, Book 4
Lucas, Book 5
Parker, Book 6
Carter, Book 7
Weston, Book 8
Greyson, Book 9
Rowan, Book 10
Caleb, Book 11
Kurt, Book 12
Tucker, Book 13
Harley, Book 14
The K9 Files, Books 1–2
The K9 Files, Books 3–4
The K9 Files, Books 5–6
The K9 Files, Books 7–8
The K9 Files, Books 9–10

The K9 Files, Books 11–12

Lovely Lethal Gardens
Arsenic in the Azaleas, Book 1
Bones in the Begonias, Book 2
Corpse in the Carnations, Book 3
Daggers in the Dahlias, Book 4
Evidence in the Echinacea, Book 5
Footprints in the Ferns, Book 6
Gun in the Gardenias, Book 7
Handcuffs in the Heather, Book 8
Ice Pick in the Ivy, Book 9
Jewels in the Juniper, Book 10
Killer in the Kiwis, Book 11
Lifeless in the Lilies, Book 12
Murder in the Marigolds, Book 13
Nabbed in the Nasturtiums, Book 14
Offed in the Orchids, Book 15
Lovely Lethal Gardens, Books 1–2
Lovely Lethal Gardens, Books 3–4
Lovely Lethal Gardens, Books 5–6
Lovely Lethal Gardens, Books 7–8
Lovely Lethal Gardens, Books 9–10

Psychic Vision Series
Tuesday's Child
Hide 'n Go Seek
Maddy's Floor
Garden of Sorrow
Knock Knock...
Rare Find
Eyes to the Soul
Now You See Her

Shattered
Into the Abyss
Seeds of Malice
Eye of the Falcon
Itsy-Bitsy Spider
Unmasked
Deep Beneath
From the Ashes
Stroke of Death
Ice Maiden
Snap, Crackle...
What If...
Psychic Visions Books 1–3
Psychic Visions Books 4–6
Psychic Visions Books 7–9

By Death Series
Touched by Death
Haunted by Death
Chilled by Death
By Death Books 1–3

Broken Protocols – Romantic Comedy Series
Cat's Meow
Cat's Pajamas
Cat's Cradle
Cat's Claus
Broken Protocols 1-4

Broken and... Mending
Skin
Scars
Scales (of Justice)

Broken but... Mending 1-3

Glory
Genesis
Tori
Celeste
Glory Trilogy

Biker Blues
Morgan: Biker Blues, Volume 1
Cash: Biker Blues, Volume 2

SEALs of Honor
Mason: SEALs of Honor, Book 1
Hawk: SEALs of Honor, Book 2
Dane: SEALs of Honor, Book 3
Swede: SEALs of Honor, Book 4
Shadow: SEALs of Honor, Book 5
Cooper: SEALs of Honor, Book 6
Markus: SEALs of Honor, Book 7
Evan: SEALs of Honor, Book 8
Mason's Wish: SEALs of Honor, Book 9
Chase: SEALs of Honor, Book 10
Brett: SEALs of Honor, Book 11
Devlin: SEALs of Honor, Book 12
Easton: SEALs of Honor, Book 13
Ryder: SEALs of Honor, Book 14
Macklin: SEALs of Honor, Book 15
Corey: SEALs of Honor, Book 16
Warrick: SEALs of Honor, Book 17
Tanner: SEALs of Honor, Book 18
Jackson: SEALs of Honor, Book 19
Kanen: SEALs of Honor, Book 20

Nelson: SEALs of Honor, Book 21
Taylor: SEALs of Honor, Book 22
Colton: SEALs of Honor, Book 23
Troy: SEALs of Honor, Book 24
Axel: SEALs of Honor, Book 25
Baylor: SEALs of Honor, Book 26
Hudson: SEALs of Honor, Book 27
Lachlan: SEALs of Honor, Book 28
SEALs of Honor, Books 1–3
SEALs of Honor, Books 4–6
SEALs of Honor, Books 7–10
SEALs of Honor, Books 11–13
SEALs of Honor, Books 14–16
SEALs of Honor, Books 17–19
SEALs of Honor, Books 20–22
SEALs of Honor, Books 23–25

Heroes for Hire
Levi's Legend: Heroes for Hire, Book 1
Stone's Surrender: Heroes for Hire, Book 2
Merk's Mistake: Heroes for Hire, Book 3
Rhodes's Reward: Heroes for Hire, Book 4
Flynn's Firecracker: Heroes for Hire, Book 5
Logan's Light: Heroes for Hire, Book 6
Harrison's Heart: Heroes for Hire, Book 7
Saul's Sweetheart: Heroes for Hire, Book 8
Dakota's Delight: Heroes for Hire, Book 9
Tyson's Treasure: Heroes for Hire, Book 10
Jace's Jewel: Heroes for Hire, Book 11
Rory's Rose: Heroes for Hire, Book 12
Brandon's Bliss: Heroes for Hire, Book 13
Liam's Lily: Heroes for Hire, Book 14

North's Nikki: Heroes for Hire, Book 15
Anders's Angel: Heroes for Hire, Book 16
Reyes's Raina: Heroes for Hire, Book 17
Dezi's Diamond: Heroes for Hire, Book 18
Vince's Vixen: Heroes for Hire, Book 19
Ice's Icing: Heroes for Hire, Book 20
Johan's Joy: Heroes for Hire, Book 21
Galen's Gemma: Heroes for Hire, Book 22
Zack's Zest: Heroes for Hire, Book 23
Bonaparte's Belle: Heroes for Hire, Book 24
Noah's Nemesis: Heroes for Hire, Book 25
Tomas's Trials: Heroes for Hire, Book 26
Heroes for Hire, Books 1–3
Heroes for Hire, Books 4–6
Heroes for Hire, Books 7–9
Heroes for Hire, Books 10–12
Heroes for Hire, Books 13–15
Heroes for Hire, Books 16–18
Heroes for Hire, Books 19–21
Heroes for Hire, Books 22–24

SEALs of Steel
Badger: SEALs of Steel, Book 1
Erick: SEALs of Steel, Book 2
Cade: SEALs of Steel, Book 3
Talon: SEALs of Steel, Book 4
Laszlo: SEALs of Steel, Book 5
Geir: SEALs of Steel, Book 6
Jager: SEALs of Steel, Book 7
The Final Reveal: SEALs of Steel, Book 8
SEALs of Steel, Books 1–4
SEALs of Steel, Books 5–8

SEALs of Steel, Books 1–8

The Mavericks
Kerrick, Book 1
Griffin, Book 2
Jax, Book 3
Beau, Book 4
Asher, Book 5
Ryker, Book 6
Miles, Book 7
Nico, Book 8
Keane, Book 9
Lennox, Book 10
Gavin, Book 11
Shane, Book 12
Diesel, Book 13
Jerricho, Book 14
Killian, Book 15
Hatch, Book 16
The Mavericks, Books 1–2
The Mavericks, Books 3–4
The Mavericks, Books 5–6
The Mavericks, Books 7–8
The Mavericks, Books 9–10
The Mavericks, Books 11–12

Collections
Dare to Be You…
Dare to Love…
Dare to be Strong…
RomanceX3

Standalone Novellas
It's a Dog's Life
Riana's Revenge
Second Chances

Published Young Adult Books:

Family Blood Ties Series
Vampire in Denial
Vampire in Distress
Vampire in Design
Vampire in Deceit
Vampire in Defiance
Vampire in Conflict
Vampire in Chaos
Vampire in Crisis
Vampire in Control
Vampire in Charge
Family Blood Ties Set 1–3
Family Blood Ties Set 1–5
Family Blood Ties Set 4–6
Family Blood Ties Set 7–9
Sian's Solution, A Family Blood Ties Series Prequel Novelette

Design series
Dangerous Designs
Deadly Designs
Darkest Designs
Design Series Trilogy

Standalone
In Cassie's Corner

Gem Stone (a Gemma Stone Mystery)
Time Thieves

Published Non-Fiction Books:

Career Essentials
Career Essentials: The Résumé
Career Essentials: The Cover Letter
Career Essentials: The Interview
Career Essentials: 3 in 1